SEDUCING
Cinderella

A FIGHTING FOR LOVE NOVEL

Praise for Seducing Cinderella

"Deliciously sexy and fabulously fun, with a hero who knocked me out from the first page!"
— USA TODAY Bestselling Author Cari Quinn

"A complete knockout—hot sex scenes, a great ending, and a hero and heroine that smouldered. Maxwell's debut was well worth the wait and can't wait to read her next!"
— *New York Times* Bestselling Author Jennifer Probst

"Seducing Cinderella is one of those books you can't put down. From the first page, Maxwell seduced me with this romantic tale featuring the hottest hero I've read in a long time. I can't wait for the next book."
— Bestselling author Candace Havens

"...a hero who is seriously molten hot while at the same time having a real sweet side...Seducing Cinderella was an all-around fun, fast-paced read! Definitely recommend!"
— *New York Times* Bestselling Author Laura Kaye

"Seriously steamy! Love Reid and Luce's story!"
— Bestselling Author Jessica Scott

SEDUCING
Cinderella

A FIGHTING FOR LOVE NOVEL

GINA L. MAXWELL

Entangled Publishing, LLC
2614 South Timberline Road
Suite 109
Fort Collins, CO 80525
Visit our website at www.entangledpublishing.com.

Brazen is an imprint of Entangled Publishing, LLC. For more information on our titles, visit www.brazenbooks.com.

Edited by Liz Pelletier
Cover design by Heather Howland

ISBN   978-1-62061-291-0

Manufactured in the United States of America

First Edition July 2012

The author acknowledges the copyrighted or trademarked status and trademark owners of the following wordmarks mentioned in this work of fiction: Barbie and Ken, MMA, YMCA, *The Piña Colada Song, Taboo!, Catch Phrase,* Transformer, Britney Spears, Jessica Rabbit, *Who Framed Roger Rabbit?, Iron Chef America,* Nordstrom, Ibuprofen, Lycra, Andes, Barnum & Bailey, Diet Mountain Dew, Puss N Boots, Shrek, NCIS, Crush, Wheaties, Pantene, iPod, He-Man, Invisible Man, *Jackson* by Johnny Cash, *Warrior, Rocky,* Nike, *Just Do It, Pinocchio,* Victoria's Secret, *The Lone Ranger, Twilight Zone,* Cherry Garcia, Disney World.

For my husband who has had to deal with my tendencies to flit from one obsession to another over the years as I searched for, and finally found, The Thing I Was Meant To Do. Thank you for not jumping off my Crazy Train, babe.

CHAPTER ONE

Lucie Miller didn't bother looking up when she heard the knock on her office door. Her next physical therapy patient was early, which irked her since she hadn't even completed the paperwork from the previous appointment. She pushed her glasses back in the proper place. He could just cool his heels in the hallway for the next ten minutes while she fini—

The knock came again, a little more insistently this time, and her resolve to not cater to someone else's wishes crumbled, as usual. Dropping her pen to the sheaf of papers in front of her, she called out, "Come in."

A head of perfectly styled dark hair popped around the edge of the door. "Hope I'm not disturbing you."

Before she could order her heart to behave,

it skipped a beat at the mellowy-smooth voice of Dr. Stephen Mann, Director of Sports Medicine and major hottie at Northern Nevada Medical Center. At warp speed, her brain performed an unsolicited catalog of her appearance, spitting out the usual diagnosis of "plain and disheveled." Holding back a disappointing sigh and the urge to smooth a hand over the strands of hair that escaped her ponytail, she gave him her best smile. "Not at all. I didn't forget another meeting, did I?"

Twin dimples winked at her. "No, not today."

He turned to close the door, and her pulse raced. As an orthopedic surgeon, he'd visited her less-than-impressive office in the Rehab and Sports Med Center plenty of times to discuss mutual patients. But not once had he ever closed the door.

Trying hard not to jump to conclusions, she gestured in front of her. "Please, have a seat."

"Uh…"

Lucie glanced to the single visitor chair piled high with file folders, old newspapers, and research articles. She swore she felt her cheeks actually change color as she bolted around her desk. "Oh my gosh, I'm so sorry. Here, let me just—"

"That's all right, you don't have to—"

"No, I insist." She gathered the haphazard

paper mountain in her arms. Not for the first time, or even the hundredth time, she wished she weren't so disorganized. Spinning in a quick circle, she searched for a place to stash the mess. Stacks just like the one she held lined the walls of her office on the floor and over every square inch of desk and file-cabinet space. Finally she gave up and just plopped the pile into her chair before turning her attention to her guest. God, why couldn't she be smooth and put-together like other women? Like the kind Stephen dated. "So, what brings you down into the bowels of the hospital this afternoon?"

He cleared his throat and shifted in his seat. Normally, the gorgeous doctor was the picture of confidence. It was the reason women literally sighed in his wake. Well, that and his easy charm and Ken-doll good looks, complete with killer smile.

"The hospital's annual charity dinner and dance is only two months away, and whereas a guy only has to rent a tux and show up, I'm aware that a woman needs ample time to shop for a dress and schedule all sorts of hair and nail appointments and whatever else it is that you women do to make yourselves beautiful."

Lucie's throat closed, and her fingers flew to fidget with her necklace. This was it. They'd worked together for years, sometimes even staying hours past their shifts to work on mutual cases, ordering bad Chinese when their brains refused to quit but their stomachs could no longer be ignored. They'd always been intellectually compatible, and their mutual obsession to help patients recover quicker and better bonded them as nothing else could. She'd loved him for years, but he'd never asked her out. Never made a move, instead preferring to date classy businesswomen he met during happy hour at the posh Club Caliente down the street.

But now he was here. In her office. Talking about the hospital ball. Dear God, please don't let her faint. Taking a slow, deep breath, Lucie tried for casual. "Are you trying to ask me something, Stephen?" And failed miserably. *Damn.*

A strong hand rubbed at the back of his neck, and he gave her the cutest look of embarrassment. "Ah, yeah. I'm not doing a very good job of it, am I?"

"No, you're doing fine!" *Too much enthusiasm. Double damn!*

"I know I should've brought this up before. And I really did want to ask that night I saw you at Club Caliente last month, but I hesitated and then you left. I was hoping I'd see you there again because it doesn't quite seem appropriate to inquire about a date here at the office, you know?"

Her mind flashed back to the one night she'd ever stepped foot in the overcrowded, overpriced club. Her best friend, Vanessa MacGregor, had just won a really difficult case and wanted to celebrate with a few drinks and some dancing. Instead of going to their usual hangout, Fritz's, Vanessa convinced Lucie to meet her at the much closer meat market of a club. They'd only been there for an hour tops before leaving. The club was like a frat house on steroids with a country-club clientele. The rest of their night had been spent downing tap beer and hustling guys at darts in a proper celebration.

"Oh, don't worry," she assured him. "I mean, not down here. The only person that could possibly hear us right now is Mr. Kramer on the treadmill out there, but the door is shut, and even if it wasn't, I don't think he remembers to turn his hearing aid up very often, so the chances of him hearing us over the noise of the mach—"

"Lucie."

"Sorry." *Oh my God, would you shut up already? You're babbling like an idiot!* "You were saying?"

He took a deep breath and exhaled like he was preparing to BASE jump from the roof of the hospital instead of asking her on a date. "I was trying to get your friend's number."

"My...*what*?"

"The girl you were with that night. Is she seeing anyone?"

"Vanessa?" Lucie's mind scrambled as it tried to follow the sharp turn off the path the conversation had previously been headed. Or where she'd *thought* it had been headed. She was such an idiot. "Um, no, she's not seeing anyone..."

Every muscle in his body visibly relaxed as he stood, his easy smile returning to hit her with both dimples right between the eyes. "That's great! Can I get her number? I don't want to take the chance of waiting till the last minute to ask her. I'd like to take her on a few dates before the big event, too. You know, get to know each other better. Lord knows you can never have a decent conversation at that charity dinner without someone interrupting with shoptalk. Lucie? Are you listening?"

"What? No. I mean, yes, I'm listening. Yes, you're right. It's definitely not conducive to first-date discussions." Lucie dropped her gaze to the organized disaster on her desk. Vanessa would have a panic attack if she saw it. Her friend was hyperorganized, always put together on the inside and out, never a hair out of place or an emotion uncalled for. Add in the perfect Barbie-doll looks and you had the kind of woman Stephen Mann was drawn to. The kind of woman she was most definitely not.

"Soooo… Can I have her number? Or maybe you're playing the role of protective friend and would prefer to grill me about my intentions first," he teased. "Maybe ask me why I think I'm good enough for her, something like that?"

She couldn't help the small lift at the corner of her mouth. "As if you couldn't be good enough for someone. You're charming, smart, handsome, and successful. How could that amount to 'not good enough' by anyone's standards?"

He winked. "I am quite the catch, aren't I? Be sure to tell Vanessa that when she tells you I called her. That is, if you ever give me her number."

"Oh! Right, sorry. Uh…" She looked around for a Post-it note or scratch piece of paper. She knew she had some, and if she could stop and think for a minute, she'd know right where they were, but somewhere in the last five minutes she'd been given a full frontal lobotomy, and now she couldn't function.

Giving up, she grabbed her pen and his hand and scribbled Vanessa's cell number onto his palm. She had to force herself to release him before she did something stupid like add an exclamation mark and "accidentally" use too much force for the dot, puncturing his smooth skin with the tip of her ballpoint. "There you go. All set. Now you'll have to excuse me. I, um, have a new patient who should be here any minute."

"I won't take up any more of your time then. Thanks, Lucie." Using his ink-free hand, he grabbed the knob and opened the door before looking back and adding, "I owe you one."

She pasted what she hoped was at least a facsimile of a smile on her face as best she could. "I'll keep that in mind, doctor."

As soon as he was gone, she sank into her chair, not even bothering to move the stack of papers before she did so. This wasn't anything new. In fact, being overlooked for someone else was typical. By now, she should be immune to the hurt that came with it. What was that phrase? Old hat. Yes, that was it. By now, this should be old hat, and it wasn't even the first time a guy she liked was interested in her friend. But it still hurt. A lot.

There was no fooling herself any longer. She would never be the object of the doctor's desire. And though the realist in her said it didn't matter—that all she needed was compatibility and companionship with someone else—as her future came into sharp focus, the dreamer in her allowed herself to shed the tears that blurred the world in front of her.

CHAPTER TWO

"Can you point me in the direction of the physical therapy department?" *Where some arrogant ass will give me exercises fit for a toddler, essentially castrating me in the process…*

To say Reid Andrews was in a foul mood was a total understatement, but that didn't mean the hospital receptionist deserved his wrath. He listened as she gave him directions and thanked her as he set off.

The closer he got to his destination, the more his muscles bunched in irritation. He shouldn't be here. He should be back in Vegas, working his injury out with his coach and team doc. Not Sparks, Nevada—which was practically Reno and way too close for comfort to his hometown of Sun Valley to the north. Now he would be working with someone who had no concept of his sport or how important it was for him to get back in the cage as soon as possible to prep for his rematch.

For as long as he could remember, he'd been fighting. Fighting in the sport he loved above all else—Mixed Martial Arts, or MMA—to get to the top, and then fighting his ass off to stay there. Fifteen years later, he was one of the richest light-heavyweight fighters in the UFC, with a record of 34-3 and a fanbase of millions. Of course none of that mattered now because if he couldn't get healthy in time for the rematch, his career was over.

A doctor talking on his cell and checking his pager crowded Reid around a corner and bumped into him. The guy didn't even look back to apologize as he continued to clip down the hallway. Reid clenched his jaw and held his right shoulder as he waited for the pain to subside. Even from an impact so small, it hurt like a bitch.

He had one of the most aggravating injuries a fighter could have: a torn rotator cuff. To literally add insult to injury, it hadn't even happened in a fight. He'd gotten the damn thing while training for his title fight. Thirty-four was almost ancient for a fighter, especially one who'd been at it for as long as he had, and his body was starting to reflect that, injury by godforsaken injury.

Sidestepping an old lady traveling at the speed

of a land snail, Reid cursed his trainer, Butch, for sending him here.

Shortly after Reid had had the surgery to repair his right shoulder, the camp's sports medicine doc needed to return home to take care of his ailing father. Scotty wasn't expected to be back for a couple of months, and since Reid was the only injured one in the camp, Butch set him up with a local PT for the interim. But if Reid kept working with that guy, he wouldn't be ready to fight until he was fifty, so he'd taken his therapy into his own hands.

Unfortunately, Butch got hip to what he was doing and bawled him out for not listening to Scotty's replacement and taking it easy. But Reid didn't know the meaning of taking it easy. His mottos were more than just your average motivational fodder. He lived by things like "give more than your everything or you'll amount to nothing" and "if you didn't come to win, you should've stayed the fuck home." Shit like that had been drilled into him since he was old enough to throw a punch at his old man's command.

He refused to accept the possibility of not completely healing in the next two months, thereby losing his shot at ever reclaiming his title. Every year the sport produced younger and better fighters, and it was becoming increasingly difficult for the older fighters to compete. That's why Reid trained as hard as he did. There would always be some guy who wanted his belt and was working his ass off for a chance to take it, so he had to train and prepare that much harder to keep it. He was pissed as hell Butch had given him an ultimatum: leave camp and do PT the right way or he was pulling the fight.

Fuck. That.

Fine, whatever. He'd make his coach happy and go to this lame PT shit. But that didn't mean he wasn't going to treat it any differently than he did his regular training. He didn't have time to dick around. He needed to get back to Vegas a.s.a.p. so he could reclaim what was rightfully his.

Reid pushed open the double doors and walked through a large room resembling the inside of a YMCA. Treadmills, ellipticals, weight sets, and exercise balls. No sparring cage. No floor mats. No punching bags. However there was an old man of about eighty-plus years walking so slow on a treadmill that he was practically immobile.

"This blows," he mumbled as he approached the small office with his PT's name, Lucinda Miller, on the partially closed door. He raised his hand to give a quick rap before announcing himself, but paused when he heard soft sniffles coming from the bowed head of a brunette sitting behind the desk. At least he assumed it was a desk. It was hard to tell what was under the stacks of files and papers. Instead of knocking, he cleared his throat. "Sorry, this a bad time?"

The woman spun her chair around to face the back wall, hitting her knee on a file cabinet in the process and muttering an expletive he'd bet she didn't use publicly very often. Though he hadn't seen her face yet, he couldn't help but find her clumsiness sort of cute. When she grabbed a Kleenex from somewhere on her floor and blew her nose, he was reminded that she was in a vulnerable moment. "I can come back."

"No, no." She blew her nose and then gestured behind her without turning around. "If you could just go have a seat in the next room, I'll be right with you."

Sounded good. As much as he hated to see a woman upset, it was bad enough having to console someone he knew, much less a woman he didn't. Finding the room, Reid leaned his hips on the padded table, absentmindedly cracking his knuckles as he waited. It was only another minute before she breezed in, eyes on his file, while making a beeline to the small desk along the wall.

"I'm terribly sorry about that," she said. "Let me just take a brief moment to look this over and we'll get down to business."

"Take your time." Something about her voice poked at his brain. Almost like he'd heard it before.

"Okay, Mr. Johnson, let's take a look at—"

They froze as recognition took hold.

"Luce?"

"Reid?"

It had been several years—shit, six, maybe even seven or more, he couldn't remember—since the last time he'd seen his best friend's little sister. Her face was blotchy with her eyes rimmed in red from crying. so he almost hadn't realized it was her, but the freckle at the outer corner of her left eye vaguely shaped like a heart gave her away. It was just barely visible under the dark-rimmed, rectangular glasses she wore.

"Oh my gosh," she said, giving his waist a hard squeeze. It'd been so long since he'd seen anyone from their hometown, and besides her brother, she'd be the only person he'd care to see. He returned her hug, tucking his head down to hers. Her hair smelled like a mix of flowers and summer, so different from the heavy perfume concoctions he was used to women wearing.

She released him, taking a seat on the swivel stool in front of the desk while tucking loose strands of hair behind her ear. "I can't believe it's you. Wait, why does my chart say Randy Johnson?"

Reid chuckled at the ridiculous name he used for anonymity. "It's an alias." Wanting to erase the pained look from whatever had happened before he arrived, he gave her a wicked smile and added, "And sometimes a state of being."

Her brows gathered together for the few seconds it took to sink in, then her cheeks flushed with color and her eyes grew wide. "Reid!"

He couldn't have stopped his laugh if he wanted to. The shocked look on her face was totally worth it. "Come on, Lu-Lu, you can't still be that innocent after all these years."

"My innocence or lack thereof is none of your business, Andrews. And be forewarned: if anyone hears you call me one of those ridiculous nicknames, I'll stab you in the jugular with my pen."

He held up his hands in mock surrender. "Fair enough, Lubert." She rolled her eyes, but he interrupted her before she could get a good mad on. "Speaking of names, what's up with Lucinda Miller? I don't see a ring. You in the witness protection plan or something?"

She averted her eyes, suddenly finding that her name tag needed repinning. "No. I *was* married briefly in college. Jackson probably didn't tell you about it because we eloped and it didn't last very long." She cleared her throat and smiled at him, but it barely reached her cheeks, much less her eyes. "You know how it is. Capricious youth and all that. I just never bothered to change my name back. But at least I still have the same initials, right?"

Her attempt at disguising her true feelings reminded him of what he'd walked in on. Something or someone had hurt her, and it instantly called on his protective instincts. After all, Lucie wasn't just any woman. He'd grown up with her trailing after him and her brother, Jackson Maris. And since Jax, also a UFC fighter, was in Hawaii with his training camp and couldn't help make things right for his little sister, Reid would gladly step in.

"Why were you crying, Lu?"

"Oh, that?" She waved a hand dismissively. "Nothing. I have terrible seasonal allergies and sometimes they get so bad I sound like a blubbering, sniveling mess, that's all."

He scoffed. "This is why Jax and I never let you tag along on our more devious 'misadventures.' You're a terrible liar and wouldn't have lasted five seconds under parental interrogation."

She stood, placing her hands on her hips. "Well according to your trainer, you're a terrible patient, so I guess we both have our faults. Now, unless you want to waste your entire session on pointless chatter, I suggest you let me assess your injury."

Reid recognized a brick wall when he ran into one. She wasn't going to talk about it…yet. One way or another he'd get it out of her. "Fine. Assess away, Luey." Reaching between his shoulder blades with his left arm, he pulled his T-shirt off over his head, taking care not to jostle his right arm too much. He tossed the shirt onto the chair in the corner.

"How much PT have you had since the operation?"

"I don't know, the usual amount, I guess. A session a day or so. But it wasn't enough, so I was doing some extra training on the side."

She paused and arched a brow at him. "In other words, you were overdoing it, which is counterproductive to your recovery."

"'Overdoing it' is such a subjective term."

"No, it's not, Reid. Anything more than what your doctor or therapist instructs is overdoing it. If I'm going to help you, you need to do *exactly* as I say. If you can manage that, I'll have you as good as new in about four months."

"What? Didn't Butch tell you about my rematch in two months? I need to fight on that card, Luce. Diaz has my belt, and I'm taking it back."

Lucie shook her head. "Reid that's insane. Even if I devoted the majority of my time to you, I can't guarantee you'll be ready to fight that soon."

"Bullshit. You have to say that as a professional, but take into account who your patient is. I'm not like the other people you work on. I'm not your Average Joe trying to eventually get back to normal. I'm a highly trained athlete who's had to recover from more injuries in the last fifteen years than a hundred Average Joes put together."

She sighed. "Let's see what we're dealing with here, first, okay, hotshot? Sit."

Reid hopped onto the table and tried not to tense up at the idea of having his arm manipulated. He had a high tolerance for pain, but that didn't mean her exam wouldn't be enough to set his teeth on edge.

"Extend your arm to the side and try to keep it there as I push it down." He lasted only a few seconds before he released the pose with a muttered curse. She pretended not to notice and put him through a couple more strength tests where he managed to keep his swearing rants inside his head. Yay him.

"Okay, last one, Reid. Place your hand in front of your stomach and try to hold it there as I pull it away from your body."

Clenching his jaw and his left fist he tried thinking of something other than the sickening pain shooting from his shoulder. But as bad as the pain was, the fact that he was so weak and couldn't hide it was much worse.

"All right, you can relax now." She made some notes in his file, then turned back and asked, "On a pain scale of one to ten, with ten being the worst pain you can imagine, how are you feeling at the moment?"

"A four. Maybe even a three."

She arched her brow and crossed her arms over her chest. "Spare me the macho shit, Andrews. I'm not here to challenge your virility. If you want me to do my job, then you have to be one hundred percent honest with me."

He pinned her with a glare that made men twice her size reconsider stepping into the octagon with him. Lucie didn't even flinch. He would've commended her for it had he not been so aggravated with the whole situation. "Fine. A six," he grumbled. "But some days are better than others."

"Don't worry, that's normal. Now lay facedown on the table. I want to do a couple more things."

"You got awfully bossy in your old age, you

know that?" He was a tad disappointed she didn't rise to the bait, but offered a sarcastic *Mm-hmm* instead as he arranged his body on the table. With his left arm up to cradle the side of his face, he let his eyes close as she began to work on him.

Her delicate fingertips probed the muscles around his shoulder. He had no idea what she was looking for, but he hoped she searched for a while. Her touch felt so much better than how he was usually handled. Of course Scotty's hands weren't as soft, but it was more than that. It was the technique she used; like he wasn't just a fighter made of hardened muscle that could handle rough, prodding fingers, but rather a man who'd asked for a gentle massage after a long day.

He heard a soft sniffle, and it set his mind to wondering what had upset her so much. Growing up he'd practically been Lucie's second older brother, and it bothered him to know something was wrong.

Whatever it was, she was doing her best to avoid— "Ah, shit!"

"Sorry."

"Yeah, right," he said wryly. "That was probably payback for using your floppy bunny as a lawn-dart target."

He couldn't see her face, but he heard the smile when she spoke. "I forgot all about that.

Jackson got grounded for three days, and my mom had to sew all the little holes together. She told me he was a war hero who was going through surgery to get patched up before receiving a medal from the president."

"Your mom was always good for a story. Jax and I counted on her to give us all our background information for our pretend missions as kids."

"Mom was something special all right. I still miss her bedtime stories."

Lucie's parents had died in a car accident the summer after he and Jackson graduated high school and she was just thirteen. Jackson chose to raise Lucie instead of pawning her off on another relative, which is why he wasn't as far in his MMA career as Reid. It was an honorable thing, and it was obvious he'd done a damn fine job, too.

Just then it hit him. "It's a guy, isn't it?"

Her hands stilled for only a moment, but it was long enough to give him the answer he was looking for. "Is it tender when I press here?"

Like bad heartburn, an unfamiliar lividity rose up for the general male population until he could aim it at the one who deserved it. Pushing up with his left arm he swung his body around to face her.

"What are you doing? I'm not done."

"You are until you tell me who he is and what

the hell he did," he growled.

"Reid—"

"Quid pro quo, Lu. You tell me who made you cry and why, and I promise to not find out on my own, hunt him down, and kick his teeth down his throat for putting that look on your face."

He almost regretted throwing down the harsh threat when her face blanched, but if that was the only way he could get her to open up, then so be it. "Here, hop up on the table. We'll switch places," he said as he stood. When she opened her mouth to brook an argument, he narrowed his gaze to show her he wasn't kidding. With a resigned sigh she did as he wanted, albeit not happily.

"There, now you're the patient." Despite the pain it caused in his shoulder, he braced his hands on either side of her hips, preventing an escape should she decide it was the better alternative. "So, Miss Miller," he said looking into her soft gray eyes, "tell me where it hurts."

• • •

Lucie still couldn't believe Reid was in her therapy room. When they were younger she'd trailed after her older brother just to be in his best friend's presence. But since Reid had always treated her like a big brother would, much to her young heart's dismay, she'd always looked up to both him and Jackson.

Now she was having a hard time looking *away* from him.

He'd always been toned in high school, but this was ridiculous. The man redefined Michelangelo's idea of perfection, making the statue of *David* look like a flabby wuss. His dark blond hair was cut close to his head and brushed forward and to the center, creating the tiniest of faux-hawks, and giving his model-perfect good looks a slight edge. Then there were the tattoos... good Lord, the tattoos.

Black tribal designs wove an intricate pattern around his upper right arm, over his shoulder and pectoral muscle, and snaked midway up the right side of his neck. Down the right side of his ribcage was the phrase Fight To Win in script letters, ending at the cut muscle that slashed diagonally to his—

"Lu?"

She met his discerning hazel eyes. "Hmm?"

"You gonna start talking, or do I have to revert to tickle torture?"

Nice, Lucie, real smooth. Get a grip, would you? It's just Reid.

She rolled her eyes and glanced away hoping he wouldn't notice the tears she barely managed to hold at bay. She smiled, needing to keep the conversation light. Needing him to *not* grill her about what happened. "I'm not eight years old anymore, Reid. Pull a stunt like that and I'll slap you with a sexual harassment suit."

Gently grasping her chin he tipped her head back to meet his gaze, and with the single use of her name, "Lucie…" the floodgates cracked to let the first tears stream down.

"God, this is so stupid. Really, it's nothing," she said, swiping at the tears angrily with her fingers.

"When a man makes a woman cry, it's not nothing."

"He didn't mean to; he doesn't even know he did. It's just…" She took a deep breath and released a shaky exhale. "I've been in love with him for years, and he's never noticed me. Not like that anyway. Just before you showed up, he asked me for my best friend's number. He wants to take her to the hospital charity ball."

"Will she go?"

"No, Vanessa would never do that to me. It hurts to know he'd seen her *one time* and ever since then he's wanted to ask her out. We've spent countless hours working together, but he just doesn't *see* me."

"Then he's obviously a blind asshole."

Lucie snorted and shook her head. "You don't know Stephen. The man has more charm in his pinky than half of Reno. He's an amazing orthopedic surgeon who always goes the extra mile for his patients. He's smart, successful, and incredibly handsome. We're so compatible. I know I could make him happy if he would just give me a chance."

"So if he's too dense to make a move, why haven't you?"

Heat immediately flooded her cheeks, and she lowered her gaze to inspect her intertwined fingers in her lap. "I can't. I wouldn't know what to say. And even if I did, and he by some miracle said yes, I…"

"You what?"

"I wouldn't know what to do," she whispered.

"Do?" He tried to think what she could mean, but came up empty. Unless…"Lucie, you've dated since your divorce, right?"

"This is stupid, Reid, let me down."

He didn't budge. "You've got to be kidding me. No boyfriends?"

"I have to tell you, Andrews, your incredulity is not making me want to open up to you on this subject in the least, so just let me up and we'll schedule you another appointment for next week."

"Okay, okay, I'm sorry," he said, placing his hands on her upper arms. He winced as fire shot through his shoulder. It hadn't been his intention to upset her more than she already was. He blinked back the pain. "Hold on, what do you mean 'next week'? Aren't we going to have daily sessions at the very least?"

"For the most part, yes. Since it is Friday, we'll start next week. Besides, you're not my only patient. I have a full schedule."

Shit, now what? He needed a hell of a lot more attention than a couple of days a week.

"Maybe you should hire a dedicated PT. You know, someone who can be with you 24/7 to work with you and keep you from overtraining. If you're anything like I remember, you have no concept of holding back."

"That's perfect. That's exactly what I need. With that type of care I can be cage-ready by fight night." He stepped back with a satisfied smile and crossed his arms over his chest. "I'll send someone over later to pick up you and your things."

• • •

She'd already hopped off the table and moved to the desk, and now her head whipped around so fast he was worried she'd need her own therapy to repair the whiplash. "*What*?"

"It only makes sense if you move in with me until I'm healed, Lu. Come on, it's not like I didn't practically live at your place when we were younger. Then we can work on my shoulder more often, and you can make sure I don't do anything stupid. And you know I'm guaranteed to do something stupid."

He watched as she crossed the small room to retrieve his shirt. "Even if the idea of moving in with you for two months didn't bother me, there's the little issue of my job."

"I'll pay you for your time off, of course. Double if you want—money isn't a problem."

She gave him the universal *get dressed* signal by slapping his shirt against his chest. "You're absolutely right; money *isn't* a problem. I have at least eight weeks of vacation time saved up since I never have a reason to take it. The problem is that the idea is ludicrous!"

Reid had to think quickly or he was going to lose this fight, and something deep down told him to *not lose this fight*. He needed her to get him where he wanted to be in two months. He was as sure of it as he was his own name. Suddenly the perfect lure came to him, and though the idea gave him equal parts excitement and anxiety, he cast it anyway.

"I'll teach you how to get your doctor if you do this for me."

Lucie had been on her way out of the exam room, all but dismissing him and his offer of being roomies, but that simple statement had her feet glued several feet before the threshold. She was hooked, now he just had to reel her in carefully, or he'd lose her and his chances for a rematch. He approached her slowly from behind as he spoke.

"I'll show you how to act, what to say… everything you need to know to make him notice you. If there's one thing I know, its women and what they do that turns men on to the point of utter distraction." Her head turned to the side. Not a big movement, but enough to let him know he had her attention. "You'll have him eating out of the palm of your hand in no time. I guarantee it."

Long moments passed in slow motion. His pulse raced in his ears as he waited for her to call him an idiot or storm off in a fit of disgust. That Jackson would skin Reid alive for teaching Lucie anything having to do with seduction should've made him think twice about his offer, but he couldn't bring himself to retract it.

She shook her head as though rejecting her own thoughts. "Sorry, but—"

Before she could finish shooting him down,

a dark-haired gentleman poked his head around the door frame. "Lucie, I'm so sorry to interrupt, but I seem to have already rubbed off the, uh," the man glanced at Reid and cleared his throat, "patient number you gave me earlier. Since I was on my way out I thought I could get it from you real quick. I brought paper this time."

What. A. Douche. It took everything in him not to pound the guy right then and there. That this guy was the one Lucie had the hots for couldn't have been more plain if she'd introduced him as Dr. Clueless Dumbass.

And he was asking her for her friend's phone number. Again.

Reid watched Lucie as she stared at the doctor for long moments, almost as though she was stuck in some internal monologue and forgot that time was still ticking away out here in the real world. When the man cleared his throat and held out a small piece of paper, she blinked back into action.

"Of course, Dr. Mann." After quickly scribbling a phone number on the paper she said, "Here you go."

"Great, thanks. I'll see you later."

Reid waited. Three seconds ticked by…seven… twelve. At last Lucie squared her shoulders, spun around, and said, "You've got yourself a deal."

CHAPTER THREE

Lucie curled into the corner of her couch, knees drawn up to her chest. She held a book in her hands, but even as her eyes scanned the lines of black type, her mind didn't register a single word.

Her stomach was all in knots. She hadn't eaten dinner she'd been so nervous. Which was flat-out ridiculous because it was only Reid. Her brother's best friend. A guy who'd practically lived at her house when she was a kid. A guy who she'd mooned after for the better part of her second decade of life…A guy who was quite possibly the sexiest man she'd ever seen and whose half-naked image must have burned itself onto the underside of her eyelids because every time she closed them, it was right there waiting for her and now he was staying in her home—

Whoa! Breathe, girl, breathe. She inhaled deeply,

held it, then let it out slowly, feeling marginally better.

Earlier she'd insisted that instead of her moving into his hotel suite, Reid move into her apartment. It didn't make sense for them both to be living out of suitcases, and this way there was less chance of him being bombarded by crazy fans. He'd shown up a half hour ago, she'd shown him to the guest room, and then left him to get settled.

Suddenly a tinny rendition of "The Piña Colada Song" burst through her quiet ruminations. She snatched her cell phone off the coffee table. "Hi, Nessie, what's up?"

"Did you seriously give Dr. Jerkface my number? Because he claims he got it from you, but I figured that can't possibly be right. I mean, I'd like to think that if the man my best friend has been crushing on for years asked her for my phone number, she would've told him to go fly a kite."

"Ness—"

"Or at the very *least*, given him an excuse as to why he couldn't ask me out."

Lucie squeezed her eyes shut and placed her head on her knees. With all the craziness of Reid moving in, she'd completely forgotten. "What happened?"

"I told him that I was dating someone but you

didn't know about it yet because it's so new."

She breathed a sigh of relief. "Thanks. I'm sorry, but he caught me off guard, and I didn't know what to say."

"When are you going to either tell him how you feel or move on?"

"Vanessa…"

"I know you don't like it when I bring this up, but come on. You can't wait your whole life for this guy to up and decide one day that he likes you."

"Yeah, I know, it's just—" Lucie heard Reid open his bedroom door down the hall. "Hey, I have to go, but I'll call you tomorrow, okay?" Before her friend could argue, she closed the phone, silenced the ringer, and set it on the table.

"Whatcha reading?"

His deep voice resonating in her usually quiet, usually very male-free home sounded out of place. She watched as he crossed in front of her wearing nothing but athletic shorts hanging low—almost *indecently* low—on his hips. At some point he must've sat in the opposite corner of the couch, but she somehow lost those moments with the distraction of his bare torso.

"You keep your mouth open like that, Lu, and you're bound to catch flies," he said with a wry grin.

Snapping her jaw shut in total humiliation, she cut her eyes back to the book in front of her that could've been written in Hebrew for all she knew. She tucked her shower-damp hair behind an ear and cleared her throat. "You should put a shirt on when we're not doing therapy."

"Why? The less I wear the more comfortable I am. I put the shorts on as a courtesy to your virtue."

She gasped. When he laughed, she realized that's exactly the reaction he'd been going for. Narrowing her sights, she chucked the book in his direction, which he easily deflected with a flick of his hand. How annoying.

"Relax, Luce. There's nothing wrong with appreciating someone's more appealing physical traits. In fact, that's lesson number one."

She snorted. "How to properly ogle someone?"

"No. How to properly get someone to ogle *you*."

Suddenly Lucie needed a drink and practically bolted to the kitchen. She was almost positive she had a bottle of wine some— *Aha*! Grabbing the corkscrew out of a drawer, she worked quickly to open and pour a large glass of the Moscato wine, and then drained it almost just as fast. And then repoured.

"Do you have wine often?"

She jumped—again—and whirled to face him, glass in one hand, bottle in the other. "Will you stop sneaking up on me like that? And, no, I don't usually drink wine. This was a Christmas gift from a patient."

"I'm not sneaking. You're jumpy. Maybe the wine isn't such a bad idea." He scanned her apartment for a minute, allowing her to down most of her second glass without an audience. "Do you have a full-length mirror around here?"

"In my bedroom, but—"

"Perfect. Let's go." He grabbed the bottle away from her and led her to her room.

"What are you doing?"

"I told you, lesson number one: dress to impress."

Lucie was afraid to ask for clarification, and instead chose to gulp some more wine. After he plopped her down on her bed, he strode over to her closet and began rifling through her clothes. She thought to object, to tell him to get away from her things, but the alcohol was already easing the tension in her shoulders, and she decided to see what he was up to.

"So tell me, Luey, what's so special about this guy? Why is he our objective and not anyone else?"

"Why is that important?" she asked, wringing her hands together as she watched his back.

"Can't I just say I like him and leave it at that?"

As he moved hangars from one side to the other, occasionally pulling a garment out, only to put it back with a muttered insult, she studied the play of muscles in his shoulders and back. She'd seen Stephen in tight T-shirts when he sometimes used the PT room for a quick workout, but he didn't look anything like Reid. Where Stephen had a runner's body, thin with lean muscle, Reid's body was the exact opposite. He wasn't large or bulky like those fake wrestlers on TV, but his medium build didn't have an ounce of fat on it, and every square inch was home to a beautifully defined muscle. It definitely wasn't a hardship watching him do anything, no matter how mundane, in his shirtless state.

"Nope. Not good enough. You're willing to do something incredibly unconventional and drastic to get this guy. So I want to know why him. I need to know what I'm working with here if I'm going to help you."

She bit her lip and wondered if she dared tell him. Not even Vanessa knew, but she supposed if she could share it with anyone, it would be Reid. After all, he was in her home for the explicit reason to help her in her quest to date, and eventually marry, Stephen. Plus, he'd be gone in a couple of months, so it wasn't like he'd be around to lord her incredibly pathetic secret over her until the end of days.

Opening up her nightstand drawer, she pulled out a crinkled magazine page. It was a full-page ad for a real estate company, featuring a picturesque colonial home with an idyllic family standing in front of it. The husband stood proudly by his wife, one arm around her waist, the other hand on his son's shoulder. Younger sister stood in front of the mom who held an infant in her arms. The quintessential American couple with two-point-five kids and their faithful shih tzu at their feet.

"Here," she said, holding out the page. "I've kept this for three years. This is what I want."

Reid turned around, took the page, and studied it with a frown in his brow. "I don't get it. Does he live in this kind of a house or something? If that's what you're getting at, I have to tell you, that's not—"

"No, not the house. The whole *thing*. The perfect life. Or almost perfect because everyone knows nothing is perfect, but I'd like to get as close to perfect as I can get and that ad screams Almost Perfect."

Reid rubbed a hand over the stubble on his jaw. "Okay, I see what you're getting at, but how does Mann fit into this?"

"Stephen is compatible with me in every way. We enjoy the same music, the same taste in movies and food. We're in the same field, so we understand how it goes when you need to work well into the night sometimes. And that also feeds into our mutual desire to help others recover from physical injuries."

Reid cut off her diatribe and handed the page back. "All right. I got it. So, you're compatible with each other. But a relationship is more than just liking the same board games. What about chemistry? Passion? Love?"

What about them? They were all inconsequential, that was what. She'd been down that road already, and it had led her straight off a cliff.

Her ex had left her a broken woman. She'd believed he loved her and truly wanted to be with her despite all their differences. He'd said their love conquered opposition. That the occasional disagreement would bring spice to their marriage.

Apparently he'd also thought sleeping with another woman a few months after their wedding would do the same thing.

She'd never felt so hurt—so *stupid*—as when she'd walked in on him having some sort of hippie tantric sex with a woman whose dreadlocks rivaled those of Bob Marley. He hadn't even had the decency to look guilty. No, he'd actually stretched out a welcoming hand and encouraged her to join them. She'd almost retched on the spot before fleeing the room, and, ultimately, the marriage.

That had been the moment she decided to never again trust that love was all a relationship needed to work. She stripped the phrase "opposites attract" from her vocabulary and vowed to not get involved with anyone who wasn't suitably compatible with her. If love eventually entered into the equation, it would simply be a bonus.

But she couldn't tell him all of that. He'd think she was crazy.

Looking down at the picture, Lucie traced a fingertip over the dark-haired man that to her represented Stephen. He even had similar features. "We haven't had the chance to discover those things yet." She placed it in her drawer and pushed it closed before pinning Reid with a confident stare. "But I know that if I could just get him to *see* me…get him to give us a chance…we'll have more chemistry than we know what to do with."

He crossed his arms over his broad chest and held her eyes for a minute or two, as if he was waiting for her to break down and admit she didn't really believe anything she just said.

But that would never happen because she *did* believe it. Totally and utterly. Finally, he broke the awkward silence.

"Luce, no offense," he said gesturing to her closet, "but your clothes suck."

It was on the tip of her tongue to defend her wardrobe, but at the last second she just sighed, her shoulders slumping forward slightly. "I know. They do, don't they?"

He scrutinized her pajamas long enough that she angled her head down, thinking something was out of place. "What's wrong?"

"Do you always wear flannel pants and baggy tank tops to bed?"

"*Not* that it's any of *your* business…" Ooh, her lips were starting to get numb. *Nice*. She grinned. "…but yes. I do." A smile spread over his face, displaying a brilliant set of straight, white teeth. "Such a pretty smile," she mused aloud.

"Pretty? I think I've just been emasculated. Okay, let's go," he said as he confiscated her wine glass.

"Hey!"

"Just a minute, I want to show you something. After that you're welcome to finish off the bottle. If I'm lucky, you're one of those girls who like to dance on tabletops when under the influence."

She was too distracted by that image to resist

when he took her by the hand and led her across the room. Picturing herself gyrating on top of a table without a care in the world made her bust out laughing. "No," she said between giggles. "I think I lean more toward sleepy than crazy when I drink wine. Sorry to disappoint you."

When they reached the antique, full-length mirror in the corner, he adjusted the angle slightly so it didn't cut him off at the neck as he stood behind her. The giddy feeling she'd had a moment ago died in her throat when she met his intense gaze in their reflection. She felt frozen in place, unable to move a single muscle, as she watched his large hands slip into her peripheral vision and make their way to the front of her body.

At first contact Lucie drew in a sharp breath. He pressed the thin cotton of her loose tank top against her stomach; the heat from his palms soaked into her skin to settle deep in her belly. Slowly his hands moved toward her lower back, his thumbs barely missing the under swells of her breasts. When they finally met at the center of her back, the material was pulled taut over her body.

"There," he said with a slight nod. "What do you see?"

She sucked her lower lip between her teeth and shook her head. She'd never been comfortable showing off her body. She didn't have the curves or the full breasts and hips that men were attracted to. Between that and his touch short-circuiting her brain—or maybe it was the wine—she couldn't deign to give him an answer more than the exhale of frustration.

"Bathing suit."

It took her a minute to respond to the randomness of his statement. If that could even be considered a statement. Maybe two words was a phrase. Or a term. Wait, what did he say? "What?"

"Where's your bathing suit? I want you to put it on so we can see your body and not the clothes you choose to hide it with."

"I'm not putting on a bathing suit."

"That's okay," he said crossing his arms. "Bra and panties'll work too."

Her jaw dropped. Was he serious? She studied the hard glint in his hazel eyes. *Shit.* "I'll get my suit," she mumbled on her way to the large dresser along the wall.

"Excellent idea. I'll wait out in the hall while you change. But Luce…" She paused midrummage through her top drawer and looked over her shoulder at him. "If you're longer than three minutes, I'm going to assume you've chickened out, and I'm coming in."

She narrowed her eyes behind her glasses. "Do you always threaten people until they bend to your every whim?"

"Of course not. I've never had to resort to threats until you," he said with a cover model smile. "Ticktock."

She grabbed a handful of rolled-up socks from the drawer and threw them at his head. Unfortunately he did his bob-and-weave thing—holding his injured shoulder and *laughing*—and managed to avoid all three cotton missiles just before he closed the door behind him.

CHAPTER FOUR

Lucie tried to be annoyed with her new roommate but found herself grinning like an idiot instead. "Pompous ass." Same old Reid. She shook her head and returned to her search for the elusive bathing suit. "Aha! Found you, you little stinker." Holding up the suit Vanessa had made her buy for their vacation, Lucie winced. *Wasn't there more to it than this?*

She did love the blue-gray color with the aqua swirly patterns, but she wished the sides weren't so high cut. They hitched up past her hip bones. Vanessa claimed it emphasized her waist more, and the plunging neckline supposedly created the illusion of a bigger bust. She'd nodded dutifully to her best friend's fashion advice, but had seriously doubted something could be made from nothing. Their vacation had been canceled at the last minute when one of Vanessa's cases went to court suddenly, so thankfully she'd never had to wear the suit.

She sighed and changed. At least it was a one-piece, which is more than she could say for anything Vanessa wore in the vicinity of a pool or beach. A minute later she stood before her tall mirror, closed her eyes, and tried to ignore the blood rushing in her ears as she called out for Reid.

The door opened with a quiet *snick*, but he didn't make a sound as he moved across the floor. The utter silence made her mouth dry and her fingers twitch by her side. Where was he? Was he trying not to laugh? Oh God, why on earth did she let him talk her into this?

Suddenly she felt his body heat radiating into her back. He was close. Very close. His breath feathered the drying strands tucked around her ear, and when he spoke, the vibrations from his voice rippled along her neck. "Open your eyes, sweetheart."

With deliberate slowness, Lucie fluttered her lids open until she was once again staring at the mirror image of herself with Reid standing behind her. His frame made her look slight in comparison. She knew all of his measurements from watching his fights. Six foot three, two hundred and five pounds, a little more when he didn't need to cut weight for a fight, with a seventy-six inch reach. The tops of her shoulders barely came up to his armpits, and if she let her head fall back, it would rest comfortably in the crook of his neck.

"Now," he said, bringing her out of her dreamy observations. "Tell me what you see."

"Strong shoulders. Solid chest. Forearms roped in muscle with just the right amount of veins to make them supersexy…"

He grinned at her in the mirror and his voice became a low rumble that shot straight to her nipples. "You think my forearms are sexy, Lu?"

"Mmm-hmmm." Why did it look like she had a dopey grin on her face? Surely that wasn't what she really looked like.

"Thank you. I can honestly say no one has ever said that to me before."

Well that was a damn shame. She was about to tell him so when he rudely interrupted her train of thought. "I meant, tell me what you see of yourself."

"Oh." Studying her reflection all she saw was a woman in a girl's body trying like hell to pull off a look far beyond the realm of possibilities. "Um. I see…" What did he expect her to say? "This is stupid, Reid. I don't want to do this anymore."

As she turned to walk away, he gripped her hips and held her in place. "I'll tell you what I see. I see a beautiful woman who hides behind insecurities that have no business living in her head." She lowered her head to gaze at the floor, but strong fingers guided her chin back up. "I see a body with flawless olive skin and subtle curves that tempt a man to close his eyes as he traces each of them like a sculptor traces his subject."

"You do?" she squeaked.

"Absolutely." Reid closed his eyes and placed his hands on her outer thighs, then slid them up in a painfully slow motion. The calluses on his palms softly abraded her skin, infusing each tiny nerve with a jolt of energy she'd never known the likes of before. "Before a sculptor can duplicate the elegance of his subject, he has to memorize her with the power of touch, instead of depending on the laziness of sight."

Lucie's lips parted as her breathing came faster and her heart pounded twice as fast. Maybe more. Reid's hands continued their exploration, spanning her waist and traveling up her sides with a firm touch that spoke of a man in control. A man who knew what he wanted, and took it without remorse.

"As his hands move over every dip, every curve, every valley…the woman's body is formed in his mind, embedded in his muscle memory, so he can recreate her even if he were to go blind."

She thought the barrier of her suit was a reprieve from the sensory overload of the skin-on-skin contact…but then his hands slid around to her belly and any sense of relief she'd had was shot straight to hell. Hands as large as his, when placed down the center of her body, easily spanned her entire torso.

She wasn't sure if it was the wine or the fact that Reid Andrews, superhot friend of her brother and the guy she'd crushed on as a teenager, was touching her so intimately that was causing the surreal, out-of-body experience. From a distance she watched as the pinky on his left hand grazed the top of her mound, just high enough to be considered innocent, but low enough to cause a clenching in her womb that had her squeezing her thighs together and biting her lip to prevent the moans that wanted to be heard. And if that wasn't enough, his right thumb was caressing a path between her breasts.

Burying his face in her hair, he inhaled deeply and let out a mix between a moan and a growl, which was quite possibly the most erotic sound she'd ever heard. "Goddamn you smell good."

Her knees trembled. The strength to stand was waning. A thick fog had blown through her mind, making clear thoughts impossible. Letting go of the last thread she had on her inhibitions, she let her head fall back and to the side as his hot breath fanned over the shell of her ear.

His hands began to clench, his fingers digging into the softness of her body. She spoke his name on a moan…

And everything stopped.

With a muttered curse, Reid took hold of her arms to steady her as he stepped away. Once assured she wasn't about to face-plant into the mirror, he scrubbed his palms down his face, then winced and held his bad shoulder. "I'm really sorry, Lucie. I— Shit, I don't know what came over me. I didn't mean for any of that to happen."

Bam! Oh, goodie. Reality was back. She waved a hand in the air and gave him a carefree *pshh* that sounded more like a horse blowing air through loose lips since she couldn't feel hers worth a damn. "Don't even give it a second thought. I'm more than tipsy so my judgment is shot, and you had your eyes closed, so you can't be faulted for your libido imagining I was someone else." Willing herself not to fall and make a further ass of herself, she walked over to retrieve her pajamas from where she'd left them on the floor.

"Lu…"

Plastering on a smile, she finally turned. There was a brief moment where she may or may not have threatened her eyeballs with a painful gouging from their sockets if they so much as strayed from his face to take in the hard-body scenery below. She may be drunk and seriously lacking in shame, but there was only so much her pride could take. "Honestly, Reid, it's no big deal. I'm just really tired. It's been a long week."

Again with the forward palm-brushing thing before he placed both hands on his hips and studied her for what felt like an eternity. "Okay, yeah, I guess we should both hit the sack. I mean go to bed. Sleep! Shit."

Yep. He sucked at this word-choice game thing. She'd have to remember never to be partners with him when playing *Taboo!* or *Catch Phrase.* "Good night, Reid."

"Night, Luce."

As soon as her door was shut, she beat the land-speed record for changing clothes while intoxicated and slid under the covers. Thankfully she'd brushed her teeth after her shower earlier because leaving her room to use the only bathroom in the apartment and taking the chance of continuing their Awkward Tango was *so* out of the question.

• • •

Reid focused on the sound of his feet hitting the belt of the treadmill, the rhythmic pounding a therapeutic soundtrack to the punishment he gave his body.

Though he'd told Lucie he planned on going to sleep, there was no way he could actually do that until he expelled the pent-up energy he'd gained from Lucie's first-lesson-gone-bad. He'd lost count of how many times the scene replayed itself in his head like a DVD stuck on repeat with no damn off button.

His eyes had been closed the whole time, but he hadn't been lying when he said that his hands would create their image in his mind. It'd been over a decade since his hands had touched any sort of sculpting medium, but they hadn't forgotten how to memorize every detail of a subject. Not by a fucking long shot.

As sweat poured down his body in a cathartic release, he tried to determine the exact moment it ceased to be a lesson and turned into something that was more about passion than anything else. Hell, if he was being honest with himself, it was probably from the moment he stepped in the room to see her in that sexy one-piece, eyes closed, and waiting on him.

She'd never been one to accentuate her body like other girls. She'd been more of a bookworm and seemed content to stand in the shadows of those who preferred the spotlight, like her brother. Growing up, she'd been like Reid's younger sister, too, considering how much time he spent at the Maris residence.

So why the hell did brotherly love suddenly feel a lot more like a lover's lust? *Shit!* He had to figure out what to do about these lessons he promised to give her or he was going to be in for a couple of hellacious months. Glancing at the odometer on the digital display, he checked his distance just as it clicked over mile number ten and brought himself down to a walk for a short cool down.

Distance. That was it. He needed to keep his distance when teaching her how to be the new her. Maybe he'd take a professorial lecturing approach next time. He could stand across the room, and she could sit on the couch and take notes. Reid laughed out loud as he pictured the ridiculous scenario. Until the Lucie in said ridiculous scenario was suddenly wearing the Britney Spears version of a school uniform and asking for a hands-on lesson in Seduction 101.

"Fuck!"

Reid punched the STOP button and hopped off the machine. Breathing fast and heavy, he let his head fall back on his shoulders and squeezed his eyes shut, but decided better of it when the haunting image returned. Looked like it was going to be a cold shower before he turned in for the night. And starting tomorrow, all lessons were going to be purely hands-*off* and at least arm's length for good measure.

CHAPTER FIVE

"Absolutely not."

Reid chuckled from his seat on the couch outside the department-store dressing room where Lucie was currently balking at the fifth outfit in a row. After their morning therapy session and his lame-as-hell one-armed workout, they'd gone out for lunch. Watching her act in public had been torture. She reacted to life rather than participated, or even instigated. When spoken to, she responded. When given something, she accepted. But when the world wasn't interacting with her, it was like she was in a bubble. She didn't even look at the people around the restaurant.

For whatever reason, Lucie acted as though it was her place not to create any more ripples in life's pool than necessary. As for Reid? He preferred the cannonball approach, but he knew that wasn't for everyone. If she wanted that asshat of a doctor to notice her, though, she needed to at least make a small splash. To do that, he'd start with changes on the outside and work his way in.

As they finished their lunch he'd told her of his plan to take her shopping for new clothes. She had of course told him under no circumstance was she clothes shopping with him, but when he threatened to burn every last boring stitch in her wardrobe, she reluctantly had a change of heart.

He'd been surprised to find not one flattering piece in her closet. It was clear she had issues with her body, though for the life of him he couldn't understand why. She was slender and fit. Her breasts were on the small side, which he supposed could make a girl self-conscious if she thought every man alive wanted a couple of Dolly Partons to play with. But she was a highly intelligent woman, so she would know that was ridiculous. Wouldn't she?

"Come on, Lucie. Let's see it." The lady assisting them had picked outfits that hugged Lucie's body rather than hid it. He'd approved of everything she'd tried on. From low-rise jeans to summer shorts, fitted button-downs to slimline tanks, she'd looked great in everything she tried on.

"No. This is too much, Reid. I'm taking it off."

Since their assistant was off helping someone else, he'd have to assume this must be the "little black dress" she insisted was a necessity in every woman's wardrobe. "Either you come out, or I'm coming in. Doesn't matter to me either way."

A sigh of exasperation preceded grumbling of what sounded like his name in mixed company with some very unfavorable threats against his manhood. And yet he smiled. He couldn't help it; she was adorable when ornery.

At last she opened the door from the dressing room and strode the few feet to stand in front of him, hands on her hips and glaring at him for all she was worth. "It's immodest."

He gave her a slow once-over and couldn't see how it could be considered even remotely immodest. In fact, he was almost disappointed in it. Though the thin material of the dress complemented her body the way a sexy nightgown would, the front of it covered her all the way up to her collarbones and didn't show any skin until it ended at midthigh.

"That's not immodest, sweetheart," he said as he leaned back against the cushions and crossed his arms over his chest. "That's called dull."

"Oh really?" Pivoting on the strappy black heels, she gave him her back…and he forgot to breathe.

Where the front of her dress had lacked, the back of it more than compensated. Her entire back was open with the exception of a single spaghetti strap that ran across her shoulder blades connecting the two sides of her dress. The material followed the lines of her back with the right side sweeping over her lower back to gather just above the back of her left hip. "Christ."

"Like I said…" She walked over to the three-way mirror and let her hands fall at her sides.

Reid moved to stand behind her. His fingers itched to trace the dip of her spine. He couldn't help but wonder how she'd react during the day, where people could see them, and without the benefit of wine. Would she pull away in shock and embarrassment? Or would she shiver and arch into his touch?

When he realized he was in serious danger of sporting wood despite his convictions from the previous night, he put his sexual thoughts in a mental guillotine hold, hoping to choke the life out of them before they ruined the dry spell he needed to continue where Lucie was concerned. *Knock it off, jackass.*

"You're not exactly giving anyone a T&A peekaboo show, Luce."

"But—"

"But nothing. Whether you choose to believe it or not, this dress is sexy and classy." His gaze dropped from hers in the mirror to study the part of her that was open for the world to see. "The back is one of my favorite parts of a woman's body. I love to trace and lick the shallow line of her spine, from the top and all the way down to the twin dimples at the base of her lower back." Reid just barely stopped himself from adding that he also loved to watch the movement of his lover's shoulder blades when he placed her hands above her head to take her from behind.

He looked up to find her eyes narrowed and scrutinizing him. "My point is, Lucie, a woman's back is graceful. Not shameful." When all she did was give him a noncommittal *uh-huh* he cleared his throat and crossed his arms over his chest. "What?"

She shook her head slightly as though she wasn't sure what to make of him. "There's more to you than meets the eye, isn't there?"

He grinned and raised a brow. "I'm not a Transformer, if that's what you mean."

That at least brought out a light chuckle as she turned to face him. "No, I mean, you're not just a fighter. You see things differently than most people. There's a very artistic side to you."

No one had ever said that to him before.

It felt like a lifetime had passed since he'd done anything but fight. Not that he didn't love his sport, but sometimes he wished it wasn't all he was. He shrugged. "I was once, I guess. My senior year of high school I tried taking shop class, but a glitch in the system put me in an art class instead. I couldn't paint worth a damn, but I learned how to sketch and draw fairly well. And then we got to the sculpting…" Reid tensed as his father's disapproval came flooding back to him. It was hard for him to think about sculpting at all anymore without the memories of his father trashing all of his supplies and the makeshift studio he'd made for himself.

"Reid?" Brought out of his thoughts, his eyes flicked up. "What about the sculpting?"

"Never mind. It's not important." Turning around, he was about to call the assistant back to help gather the outfits, but Lucie grabbed his hand to stop him, placing herself square in his line of sight again.

"Yes it is. I can see it in your eyes. It's important to you. Please tell me."

Her words, combined with her fingers pressing into the center of his palm, were like an infusion of mental cortisone. It wouldn't fix the problem, but it numbed the pain just enough to get the job done. Taking a deep breath, he told her what he'd only ever told Jax. "I enjoyed sculpting. I liked that I could create with the same hands I used to destroy my opponents in the cage. You're right. I do see things differently. I don't just see an apple, but I see the individual curves and lines that make up that apple, including the bruise on one side that makes a flat spot roughly the size of a thumbprint.

"But people don't want to know that about me. They want to know what I'm doing to cut weight, what new routines my trainers are putting me through, and whether or not I think I'm going to come away with my hand raised in my next fight. It's what I'm good at. It's who I am."

"You're wrong, though," she said, taking a small step forward. "Who you are isn't just one thing. It's everything you're passionate about. You can be a sculptor, Reid, and still be a fighter if that's what you want."

The tenderness in her conviction made him want to hold her in his arms and kiss that heart-shaped freckle at the corner of her soft gray eyes. Eyes that saw remarkably through his bullshit and glimpsed his soul.

"You know what I want? I want to eat." He caught the attention of their sales lady with a wave of his arm. "Help her with the tags on this one, please. She's wearing it out of the store. Then we'll take everything else she tried on. Thanks."

When he handed over his credit card, Lucie pinned him with a glare. He was glad she wore her contacts today. She looked all hot-librarian in her glasses, but he preferred this unobstructed view of her expressive dove-gray eyes. Even if their current expression said she was clearly pissed off.

"Now what's wrong?"

She crossed her arms under her breasts and lifted her chin. "I might not be a big-time UFC celebrity like yourself, but I'm far from indigent. I'll pay for my own clothes."

Of all the things he'd expected her to say, that wasn't even in the bunch. Reid wasn't used to women who insisted on paying for themselves when they were with him. He had more money than he knew what to do with from his fights and product endorsements. That she even wanted to buy the clothes *he* insisted she get in the first place spoke volumes of her character.

"Luce," he said, pulling her arms down so he could hold her hands, effectively breaking the body language that would remind her of her anger. "I know you can buy your own clothes. You're a successful, strong, independent woman who doesn't need anyone to take care of her."

The fire in her eyes fizzled a little as he worked to break through her guard. "That's right,

I don't."

"However, the new wardrobe was my idea, so I'm going to buy you the clothes, and then I'm taking you out to dinner." She was just about to argue—it seemed to be the woman's favorite past time, for chrissakes—so he placed a finger on her lips and said, "No arguments. I'm going to head over to the men's store and get something more appropriate than these cargo shorts and polo. And grab some ibuprofen for this damn shoulder. Wait here and I'll be back to pick you up."

He removed his finger and turned to leave when he heard, "But—"

With a growl of frustration he grabbed her by the nape and pulled her against him as he planted his lips on hers. She stiffened and a shocked squeak came from somewhere in the back of her throat. But a moment later the squeak became a tiny moan and her body melted into him. Deep in his mind, his conscience screamed the words "hands-off approach," but his libido was quick to tackle it to the mat, knocking the wind out of the suddenly unwelcome reminder.

Her lips were warm under his and tasted of her strawberry lip gloss. He bet her tongue would taste just as ripe and sweet, but instinct told him if he crossed that line, he might not stop. Before he lost himself to the primal need urging him to push her into the nearest dressing room and show her how good the dress would look on the floor as well, he broke the kiss to see a dazed look on her face. "Damn, woman, do you always have to argue? Just go along with the plan or my next tactic will be public spanking."

Lucie gasped and stepped away from him as her cheeks flushed to match her ruby, just-been-kissed lips. Apparently the idea of his hand on her ass was just the image she needed to scare her into compliance. Or was it? Upon closer inspection he swore he saw glazed lust in her eyes. Could it be that his innocent Lucie had a little devil in her?

Fucking hell. Just the thought had him hardening behind his fly. He needed to get out of there. Fast. When he spoke, he was surprised by the gravel in his voice. "I won't be long." Then he spun on his heel and strode out to find the closest men's store…and enough time to lose the hard-on he was currently sporting for his friend's little sister.

CHAPTER SIX

Lucie couldn't remember a time when her nerves were more frayed. Her stomach felt so twisted inside out she thought for certain if she looked down she'd see a knotted mess where her normally flat abdomen should be.

Reid led her gently with a large hand at the *mostly bare* small of her back through the maze of restaurant tables until the hostess indicated which was theirs. After holding her chair while she seated herself, he walked around the linen-draped square table to his place across from her.

She marveled at how graceful he moved and how at ease he was in the expensive clothes he'd bought for their evening out. His white, fitted dress shirt hugged his frame, clinging to his muscles with every movement. And even though they were at a five-star restaurant, she loved how he didn't completely pander to the dress code, leaving the top few buttons undone and leaving the shirt untucked over dark dress jeans.

With his hair brushed forward and up, creating that hint of a peak down the centerline of his head, and his tattoos faintly visible through the material of his shirt, he was the epitome of a bad boy out on the town. The exact opposite of her taste in men. And yet somehow she found him utterly delectable.

Just like his kiss.

Lucie quickly picked up her menu to hide the heat flooding her face at the memory of his lips on hers. She knew he'd done it just to shut her up—that there'd been nothing sexual about it for him—but the moment his mouth touched hers the world around her became hyperfocused to exist solely on his lips. Her reaction to such a small, intimate gesture had startled her, to say the very least.

"So what are you in the mood for?" he asked.

Clearing her throat as delicately as possible, she lowered her menu and picked the first thing she saw. "Chicken Marsala sounds good."

"That does sound good, but I'm more of a steak man." The waiter approached and asked for their drink order. "I'll have a whiskey sour, and my sister would like a bottle of your Moscato wine, please."

The waiter couldn't have been any older than twenty-two to her twenty-nine, but he gave Lucie an inviting smile, winked, and said, "My pleasure. I'll be right back with your wine."

Stunned, Lucie waited until he was out of earshot before she spoke. "If it's so embarrassing to be seen with me in a place like this, you shouldn't have brought me."

The hand holding his water glass froze halfway to his mouth and his brows drew together. "Why in the hell would I be embarrassed to be seen with a beautiful woman?"

"Yeah, right." She snorted and busied herself with unfolding the dark napkin from its impossible origami-style design. Why did restaurants want to make a person feel inept before their drinks even arrived? "I see the types of girls you and Jackson date. They're the MMA's equivalent of the rodeo buckle bunnies. Big-breasted bombshells who probably hold master's degrees in Bedroom Acrobatics." After placing the finally unfolded napkin in her lap, she looked up to see Reid still had the audacity to look perplexed. She sighed and explained, "You made it a point to call me your sister in front of that waiter because you don't want your dating stable tarnished with a Plain Jane like me."

Lucie swore she heard him actually growl and if the look on his face was any indication, it seemed as though she may have indeed poked the sleeping bear. "Let's get one thing perfectly clear," he said, setting his glass down. "I don't want to hear the term Plain Jane in reference to you ever again. *Any* man, myself included, would be proud to have you on his arm."

Though she recognized his reaction as a protective thing, much how Jackson would have been, the conviction in his voice touched her... until another thought reared its ugly head. *Stephen doesn't see it that way.*

As if reading her mind, he added, "And soon that doctor of yours will get his head out of his ass and realize it, too." He paused to flick his napkin into his lap without any trouble. "But for now, you need to flirt shamelessly with the waiter."

"*What*?" she stage whispered while leaning over the table. "You can't be serious."

"I'm dead serious. Did you see the way his attitude toward you changed the moment he found out you weren't my date? He damn near drooled on our table."

"You're out of your mind. No." She shook her head. When all he did was give her that annoying *Oh, really* look she barely stopped herself from flinging a fork at his forehead. "What in God's name will flirting with a stranger accomplish?"

"Multiple things, but first and foremost, it's going to show your date that you're desired by others. Here's lesson two: Men always want what they can't have, or what other men want. It's a scientific fact."

"No it's not."

"Well, it should be," he said with a grin.

"Even if you're right, I don't know *how* to flirt, Reid. So this won't work." Wasn't it typically cold in restaurants? She was close to burning up. Maybe she was coming down with something. She reached for her ice water and took several long gulps, trying to numb herself from the inside out.

"That's what I'm here for, sweetheart. Now, there are two types of flirting. Body language and banter. Tonight I just want you to try using body language. You could recite a Mother Goose nursery rhyme, but if you give off the right signals, the guy won't stand a chance."

A teeny snort escaped, but she quickly composed herself. Clearing her throat she said, "So what exactly am I supposed to do? Flip my hair and giggle in a high-pitched voice at everything he says?"

"Only if you're looking to attract the captain of the high school football team."

She gave him her best evil eye, hoping he'd

drop this whole ridiculous notion. Fat chance.

He leaned in, resting his forearms on the table and clasping his hands in front of him. "It's easy, Lu. Carry on the conversation like you would normally, but add in subtle things. Make eye contact with him and hold it. When your eyes dart around, it tells people you're nervous or uncomfortable. You want to show confidence."

"That's all? Eye contact? I can do that."

"No, that's not all. You need to draw his attention to all those beautiful assets you have." She rolled her eyes, but he ignored her and continued. "To draw attention to your eyes, you hold his gaze or give him quick glances from under your lashes. Guys go nuts when a woman plays coy."

Lucie thought about all the times she'd seen women do that exact thing when talking to Stephen and how he'd smile back as though they were somehow having sex in their brains. She'd never attributed anything to the actual body language, though. Since she'd always been an intellectual, she'd assumed it was what they were discussing that forged that connection.

She barely restrained from slapping herself in the forehead. She'd been such an idiot. But no longer. Sure, it kind of irked her that she had to resort to using physical wiles to get a man's attention. After all, it was the intellectual things she appreciated about Stephen, and she'd hoped it would be the same for him. But once she got his attention and he felt that spark with her, the rest would surely fall into place. The idea of learning how to make that connection with Stephen was starting to excite her.

"Coy, got it. What else?"

"Draw his attention to your mouth by smiling, eating, drinking, nibbling on your lip, licking your lips…actually it's not real hard to get him to focus there since one of the first things a guy thinks of is what a girl's mouth will look like around his—"

"Reid!"

He leaned back and laughed, a rich, throaty sound that didn't do anything to help cool her down. She mentally added "laughing" as a way of drawing attention to one's mouth as her eyes transfixed on his full lips framing those perfectly straight, white teeth. And staring at his mouth only served to remind her of the searing kiss he gave her at the store, which then made the temperature in the room escalate another few degrees. *Crap!*

"Okay, here comes your boy with our drinks. He'll wait for you to approve the wine. I want you to channel Jessica Rabbit and give him a show."

Her jaw dropped. "You want me to channel

a cartoon character from *Who Framed Roger Rabbit*?"

Reid's expression actually looked like he couldn't believe her incredulity at his choice in sex goddess. "She's sex on heels. *Every* dude wants to bang Jessica Rabbit."

He was utterly insane; that's all there was to it. Her knee-jerk reaction to argue with him was cut short by the arrival of their waiter. He set Reid's drink in front of him without so much as a glance in his direction. Then he presented the bottle of wine to Lucie, rattling off the year and vineyard as if she'd know the difference between that and the stuff that came out of a box, and poured a small amount for her to taste in her glass.

Okay, I can do this. I can. *Jessica Rabbit…slow, deliberate movements, bedroom eyes…no sweat. Oh, God, I'm sweating.*

Trying her best to ignore the drop of perspiration she felt slide between her breasts, she slowly picked up the glass, held the waiter's gaze, and tipped the wine to her lips to take a small sip. The sweet wine flowed over her tongue and spread its warmth down her throat and into her belly. She let her lids drift closed and emitted a satisfactory moan before pulling the glass away. Opening her eyes again, she smiled and asked, "I'm sorry, what was your name again?"

"Daniel." He swallowed hard, his Adam's apple bobbing in his throat. "My name is Daniel."

She toyed with the ends of a section of her hair and threw him what she hoped was a dazzling smile. "Well, Daniel, the wine is lovely, thank you. Though he's usually fairly clumsy, I'm certain my brother will be able to refill my glass while you take care of your other customers. We'll be needing just a few more minutes to decide."

Daniel performed a shallow bend at the waist, returning her smile. "Of course. I'll be back shortly to take your order. And please, if there's anything I can do for you, don't hesitate to ask."

As soon as he left, Lucie downed the rest of the wine in her glass in one shot. Meanwhile, Reid was giving her a subdued slow clap. "Brava, sweetheart. You could've asked him to lick your shoes and he'd have thanked you for the opportunity. How did that feel?"

"Awful," she grumbled while he refilled her glass.

"Come on. I know it's not your comfort zone, but be honest with me." He leaned forward, forearms crossed on the table. "Be honest with yourself."

She treated herself to a few more gulps of wine and welcomed the feeling of it swirling in her veins, easing the tension in her body. Placing the glass on the table, she met his gaze and thought about what he said.

He was right. She wasn't being honest.

"It was…flattering. Empowering."

"Exactly. Remember, even when you land a date with the doc, there's nothing wrong with a little outside flirting to remind him he's not the only fish in the sea. Now, let's get your boy toy back over here, 'cause I'm starving."

The rest of the evening passed with great conversation and secret chuckles at Daniel's continued state of enamor with Lucie. When he gave Reid the check, he slipped her one of the restaurant's business cards with his number scrawled on the back. As silly as it sounded, a rush of giddy excitement flowed through her. It was the first time anyone had blatantly hit on her.

She would've kept the card, possibly laminated it and tucked it into the frame of her bedroom mirror, but Reid confiscated it, tore it in quarters, and left it on his plate. She was about to object when he said, "We're fishing for orthopedic surgeons, remember? Little ones like waiters, we throw back in. Besides, he didn't pass big brother's inspection."

Lucie couldn't help but laugh. Whether it was good food, good wine, good company, or a combination of all three, she was feeling fantastically relaxed. Something she rarely felt in public. Turned out a little dose of confidence was addictive, and she was already looking forward to getting more.

Reid stood and held his hand out to her. "Come on, let's get out of here."

She smiled and slipped her hand into his and they retraced their path from earlier toward the exit. When they passed through the waiting area she heard a child exclaim, "Dad, look! It's Reid Andrews!"

Turning she saw a boy not more than ten years old run up to them with a look of pure awe on his adorable face.

Reid held out his fist for the kid to bump his knuckles against it. "Hey, little man, how's it going? You a UFC fan?"

"Totally! You're my favorite fighter!"

Just then the boy's dad approached. "Sorry to bother you, Mr. Andrews. I thought Austin was seeing things, but it's really you. We're huge fans."

"Please, call me Reid. I'm always happy to meet fans. Do you train at all Austin?"

"Uh-huh. Right now I'm a purple belt in Tae Kwon Do, but I want to learn all the different Martial Arts so I can be like you when I grow up."

"Well, you keep training and work hard and I have no doubt you can do exactly that. Just remember that the skills you learn are to be respected and never used against others outside of the dojo."

"I know. My sensei tells us the same thing. I can't *believe* it's really you! Man, I wish my friends were here. They're never going to believe I met you."

"Tell you what, let my lovely date take a picture of you, me, and your dad. That way you have solid proof."

"Yeah!"

Lucie was so moved by the way Reid was indulging the young boy she almost didn't realize he was speaking in reference to her. "Oh! Yes, that's a great idea. Would you like me to use your phone?" she asked the father.

The man's face fell as he looked at his son. "Sorry, kiddo, but I left my phone at home so we wouldn't be interrupted at dinner." He went on to explain to Reid, "I only get him every other weekend, so I don't like anything interfering with our time together."

The disappointed look on the boy's face was enough to rip her heart out. "How about I take the picture with my phone and then I can e-mail it to you. Would that work?"

"Yes, it would. Thank you so much."

Reid posed with the boy and his dad for a nice picture in front of the gigantic fish tank, and then he suggested a fun picture with just him and Austin. She laughed as Reid crouched down to Austin's level and they held up rocker hands and donned some sort of fighter face with their noses scrunched up and their tongues hanging out.

After getting the e-mail address and ensuring both pictures had no problems sending, they said their good-byes to Austin and his dad and left the restaurant.

As they walked to the car she studied him from the corner of her eye. Suddenly he stopped and bent to pick up a discarded bag of food from the ground she'd been about to step on. Telling her to hold on, he jogged back to the entrance and tossed it into the garbage can.

When he returned she said, "That was really wonderful of you, Reid."

"What, that? I didn't want you to step on it. Besides, I can't stand littering. It's lazy, and I hate lazy people who, for instance, refuse to put forth the little bit of effort it would take to throw something away properly."

"I was talking about what you did for Austin and his father."

"Oh, that," he said, smiling. "I'm not as benevolent as you think, Lu. I get just as much of a kick out of meeting them as they do me. Especially the kids."

"Don't you worry about the impression extreme fighting could make on young children?"

He slipped his hand into hers, and she was surprised at how natural it felt. "A lot of people have issues with the sport of MMA. They call it human cock fighting. But they don't pay attention to the extreme discipline and technical aspects of what we do, or the incredible sportsmanship it takes to shake the hand of a man who just literally beat the shit out of you. As long as kids are made aware of those things, like Austin obviously was, there's nothing to worry about." He shrugged. "There'll always be people who misunderstand it. But I'd like to think they're the minority."

They arrived at his car and like the gentleman he was, he opened her door. Before climbing in she turned, tilting her head a little to the side as she studied him. "You really love it, don't you?"

"I'll always love the sport." For a moment he raised his eyes to the horizon before returning his attention to her with a bit of a sad smile. "How much longer I'll love being in it remains to be seen."

It bothered her a great deal to see him without his usual passion shining through, giving her the sudden urge to console him with a kiss. She'd intended for it to be on his cheek, but the wine must have messed with her aim because she landed square on his luscious mouth.

For several seconds they stayed like that, frozen in time, lips pressed together, until the sound of someone's car alarm brought her senses back. She pulled away and touched her fingers to her lips as if she'd just been caught doing something scandalous.

"Not that I'm complaining," he said, "but what was that for?"

She studied her feet in the strappy heels before looking up from under her lashes. "Because you're a good man. And to thank you for a wonderful day."

His wicked smile was breathtaking under the light of the moon. "Well then in that case, Miss Lucie Miller, I'm going to make sure you have a whole slew of wonderful days."

Lucie laughed and climbed into the car, but her amusement screeched to a halt before he even made it around the car. *If that wasn't her most recent lesson in high-def, she didn't know what was.* Yep, she'd just witnessed a master flirt at work. And totally fell for it hook, line, and sinker.

Now she knew what it felt like for those women who Stephen turned his charm on for. She couldn't wait to be on the receiving end of his dimpled smile. The one that said he couldn't wait to devour his latest catch instead of the buddy version she'd always gotten. Yes, sir, the doctor wasn't going to know what hit him the next time he saw her. She could hardly wait.

CHAPTER SEVEN

Lucie couldn't believe it had already been a week since Reid moved in. The days had been a whirlwind of physical therapy sessions for him and beautification appointments for her. She'd had her hair trimmed with some long layers added in, which she really liked and had felt foolish for worrying about so much. It wasn't until they did the foil highlights, making her into an aluminum Medusa, that she had an anxiety attack. Thankfully the girl knew her stuff and the subtle caramel streaks gave her darker brown a beautiful depth she hadn't known was possible.

After that her brows were waxed, shaped, and plucked to the extent she thought her eyes would never stop watering. When it came time for her nails she'd had to admit to never doing anything other than trim them when they got too long, which made the nail technician place a hand over her heart and look at her like she was a charity case off the streets before setting to work. Now they were filed, devoid of excess cuticles—she hadn't even known that was a *thing*—and polished a dark purple called Extreme Eggplant that sounded less like a color and more like a dish on *Iron Chef America*.

On top of all that, Reid handed her over to Trixie at the Nordstrom's makeup counter with instructions to give Lucie a How-To for every possible life situation. After learning how to apply everything from a five-minute dash of color to an evening look to a dramatic photo shoot session, Lucie was confident she could moonlight as a makeup artist for a morgue or circus if the economy tanked. Though some of the lessons were obviously unnecessary, she gave Trixie her head and let her have fun. Her excitement had been too endearing to crush with the reality that only a quarter of what she taught would ever see the light of day. Or night.

However, at the end of the week, Lucie had to admit that she looked almost…beautiful. It was crazy the difference some slight adjustments in her beauty regimen could make. Or, to be more exact, acquiring any sort of beauty regimen at all.

"Gorgeous."

Lucie spun around from the full-length mirror in her bedroom to find Reid leaning against the doorjamb, arms crossed over his chest, the elastic cuffs of his black polo stretched to their limits over his biceps. The deep arcs and swirls of his tattoo seemed to extend from his shirt, making it look more like futuristic armor rather than a mere cotton blend. His dark jeans encased his muscular thighs and fell straight to bunch at the hem around his bare feet. She'd learned over the last week that he didn't put socks or shoes on until he absolutely had to. And with that came the accompanying lesson of how sexy a man in jeans and bare feet was.

He pulled off the polished bad-boy look flawlessly. His hair was brushed into his usual style, but tonight the tips ended in a small peak over his forehead drawing her attention to his intense eyes. Tonight he wore earrings; square-cut diamonds that somehow managed to make him more manly, not less. When she'd cataloged every last detail and finally let her brain acknowledge the whole package, her mouth dried up and she had to swallow hard before she was able to speak.

"You look pretty good yourself," she said. "But I still don't know why you want to come to Lizzie's baby shower with me." Lizzie was one of the best nurses on staff at NNMC and was a month away from having her first child, so her friends and coworkers were throwing her a shower at a swanky steakhouse. "You're going to be bored out of your mind."

He pushed off the frame and crossed into the room. "I'm never bored. I always manage to entertain myself one way or another. Come on, we're already going to be late."

Lucie glanced at the clock on her nightstand, confirming their tardiness. "Crap!"

He chuckled as she raced to her closet to snatch her heels and purse. "Relax. Cinderella's supposed to be late to the ball so everyone notices her when she walks in."

"That's exactly what I'm afraid of," she said as she hopped on one shoed foot while trying to make the other side match with little success.

"Here, let me." Reid took the silver shoe from her and lowered himself to one knee. She stood holding onto the bedpost, mesmerized by his hands as they helped slip the shoe on her foot. The warmth of his fingers as they grazed her ankle sent shivers up her leg and spread through her sex as though he'd touched it directly.

He held her foot on his thigh with one hand while the other opened, releasing a silver chain he'd been hiding in his palm to dangle from where he held the end. Surprise left her speechless as she watched him wrap it around her ankle and clasp it in place.

The delicate chain was practically weightless, and she wondered if she'd feel it at all if it wasn't for the charm and beads attached to the small links. In the front, a small silver bird in flight hung from the chain. Crystalline beads of sky blue dangled every inch or so, completing the piece with a classic beauty.

"It's beautiful," she said. "But you've gotten me so much already, Reid. You don't need to keep getting me things."

"I know, but as soon as I saw it I thought of you."

"Really? Why?"

"This is a sparrow." He looked down and fingered the bird charm. "Unlike most birds, when a sparrow finds its soul mate, they stay together until the end of their life." Raising his head again he met her gaze. "Making them the symbol for finding one's true love."

Finding one's true love. Lucie merely wanted to find her one true companion and wasn't holding out much hope for the love part anymore. Regardless, the sentiment was the sweetest thing she'd ever heard, and knowing he'd thought of her when he saw it touched her deeply.

He carefully placed her foot back on the

floor and rose to tower over her at his full height. She tried thanking him but the words got stuck somewhere in her throat as her gaze traveled up from the open V of his shirt revealing the tan skin at his neck, past his freshly shaven jaw and full lips, until it was trapped by his eyes. They changed color depending on his outfit or his surroundings or even the lighting. Now they were a light green shot through with streaks of caramel, reminding her of a taffy apple.

Reid Andrews was an absolute enigma. In Vegas she knew he lived the life of a rich playboy fighter, spending the majority of his time either training or casually "dating" more women than she cared to think about. But since he'd moved in with her for this truly crazy deal they'd struck, he'd been nothing but charming, supportive, and thoughtful. Just like she remembered him to be when she was young and hopelessly crushing on her big brother's best friend. If she'd thought he was fantastic back then, he'd grown to be even more so now.

She cleared her throat and gave the whole speaking thing another shot. "Thank you, Reid. I love it."

"You're very welcome. Now let's go. I can't wait to see that doctor's jaw unhinge when he sees what he's been missing out on." When she scrunched up her nose in doubt, he kissed it and said, "Trust me," and grabbed her hand to lead her out of the room.

Thirty minutes later they arrived at the restaurant and the hostess escorted them back to the rented-out room where the shower was being held. Lucie placed her gift for Lizzie on the designated table by the door and then nervously scanned the sea of people.

"Stop fidgeting," Reid said in her ear. His hand at her lower back helped to ease her, but not by much.

"I'm not fidgeting."

"Yes, you are."

He was right. She was practically hyperventilating, which was likely to come next. She couldn't seem to stop. Why did she feel like she was stepping into the lion's den? These were people she'd known and been comfortable with for years. But what if they didn't like her new look? Or what if they thought poorly of her for changing her appearance?

She barely managed to keep her startled squeak contained in her chest when Reid yanked her out of the room. "Hey!"

"Shh," he ordered as he dragged her down a hall, turned a corner, and then sandwiched her between his large body and the wall. "You're freaking yourself out for no reason, so I'm going to teach you a trick I use before a fight."

"Reid, I hardly think—"

"No thinking. Visualizing. Before I step into the cage I visualize every punch, every kick, every takedown. I know my opponent well from studying his previous fights. I anticipate how he'll react to my attacks so I'll be ready for any situation. That's exactly what I want you to do right now."

She knew she must be looking at him like he was crazy, because that's exactly what she was thinking. How could this technique help her talk to Stephen? If she needed to anticipate the guy's punches, there was a bigger problem than wanting a date.

"Close your eyes." Seeing his determined look—and in all honesty desperate to try anything to get rid of her nerves—she obeyed. "I want you to picture yourself walking into that room, your head held high, and your confidence even higher. You *know* you look fabulous. This dress fits your body like it was designed for you. The heels make your legs look impossibly long and every guy in that room will be picturing them wrapped around his waist."

She was slightly cold with the A/C blasting from the vent above them, but when he placed his hand on her waist, any chills disappeared from the heat of his touch. He stepped into her body, her breasts lightly grazing his hard chest with every breath she took. Her eyes remained closed, but the magnitude of his presence was palpable. Focusing was definitely no longer an issue. She was wired into him now, brain and body, whether she wanted to be or not.

"Pretend I'm him. I haven't been able to keep my eyes off you since the moment I saw you. I'm wondering how I could've been so blind not to have noticed how truly gorgeous you are."

Reid's hand slowly slid up her side until his thumb was millimeters away from her breast. She told herself she shouldn't feel disappointed when he moved it around to her back, managing to avoid anything inappropriate. His voice, pitched low and near her ear, rolled over her skin causing the tiny hairs at the back of her neck to stand on end. "I start with simple chitchat, shoptalk, but the entire time you're talking I'm staring at your lips and imagining what they'll taste like."

"You are?" she asked on a breathy whisper.

"Fuck yeah, I am." His free hand came up to frame her face, and he nudged her cheek with his nose until her head angled to the side. "You're sexy as hell, Lucie, and I want to unwrap you to get to the decadent prize underneath. I want to learn your likes, your dislikes—to know your fears and your dreams—and I vow to peel back each beautiful layer until I discover everything about you."

Lucie's heart was pounding so hard she was sure the hostess could hear it in the front of the restaurant. She wanted to be known like that—physically, emotionally—desperately.

"Yes," she said. "I want that."

"Then *take* what you want." His voice was little more than a rasp at her ear. It sounded strained and on the edge. "Make it happen."

She was so wrapped up in the image in her mind, she didn't notice Reid had stepped back from her until the feeling of bereftness came over her. Letting her eyes flutter open, she focused on Reid standing in front of her. His hands shoved into his front pockets and the stiff look on his face didn't match the sultry emotions he'd just poured over her.

"All you have to do is remember everything I've just told you, and walk through that door." Before she could ask him if everything was all right, he jerked his head in the direction of the banquet room. "Go on. It's time to make your entrance, Cinderella."

The idea of walking into a room with all eyes on her no longer sent her into a panic. He was right. She might not be celebrity beautiful, but she did look one hundred percent better than she had a week ago. There was no reason she shouldn't find some confidence in that. Stretching up on her tiptoes Lucie placed a kiss on his cheek. "Thank you, Reid."

One side of his mouth quirked up. "Anytime, sweetheart."

With her newfound conviction and brand-new look, Lucie pushed her shoulders back and strode down the hall.

. . .

Reid dragged his hands down his face as soon as Lucie turned the corner. What he wouldn't give for a sweaty gym and a tough sparring partner to beat him senseless right now. The visualization technique was something that could be applied in any situation, so he knew it would work for her. What he hadn't known was how it would work him *over*.

He couldn't even say for sure who he'd been speaking as that whole time. At some point it felt like he'd slipped out of character. He hadn't been picturing Dr. Dipwad staring at her lips and kissing her. He'd been picturing himself.

"I need a drink," he mumbled, making his way to the room. As soon as he crossed the threshold he spotted Lucie. Like she was the North his gaze would always point to. The simple, pale blue shift dress she wore was understated and yet magnificent. He kept eyes on her as he crossed to the table set up with punch and premade cocktails. Grabbing one of the drinks he watched her ass as it moved under the thin material with every step she took. His gaze drifted lower to wander over the curves of her smooth legs. *Damn, she's hot.*

He raised the glass then stopped. If he had to guess based on the shower's signature drink, Lizzie was due to have a girl. It looked like a crazy version of a Shirley Temple, bright pink with cherries stabbed on an open plastic diaper pin straddling the rim of the glass.

"It's emasculating, isn't it?"

Reid glanced to his left to see a well-built Hispanic guy standing next to him with an amused smirk on his face. He was holding two open bottles of Corona instead of the current embarrassment he held.

"There's not even any alcohol in that thing," the guy said.

"Holy shit, that's inexcusable." He put it back on the table with a disgusted look at the whole setup. "How can they justify that?"

The man laughed, and held out the extra beer.

"It's a baby shower, man. That's all the excuse they need to suck anything even remotely manly out of the occasion. Normally we aren't even supposed to step foot in these things, but Lizzie's kind of like the darling of the hospital staff. Everyone loves her so it became an 'everyone' event. I'm Eric."

"Reid." Gladly accepting the offered bottle, he shook Eric's hand before downing half of it in one shot. "Thanks, man, you're a lifesaver."

"Don't mention it."

Looking past Eric he saw Lucie break a hug with a very pregnant girl and then walk toward her doctor who was talking with another gentleman at a table across the room. Dressed in an expensive suit and his dark hair gelled and combed to the side, he looked like the stereotypical trust-fund baby. Someone who'd always had money even before he became a doctor and was very comfortable with the finer things in life.

The doctor was in midsentence when he noticed Lucie. It was a true record-scratch moment. He did a small double take and his eyes damn near popped out of his head while his tongue rolled out of his mouth onto the floor like one of those old cartoons.

But Reid couldn't blame the guy. Lucie was in

rare form. She was crossing the room with obvious intent. A huntress approaching her trapped prey with a hint of a knowing smile at the corner of her mouth. He could almost hear her saying, *Nowhere to run…I've got you now.*

Mann excused himself from the table without even sparing the guy he'd been talking to a courtesy glance. In two steps he'd closed the distance between himself and Lucie. Though he wasn't a lip-reader, Reid could guess how the conversation was going.

Lucie, you look positively stunning!

Why, thank you, Stephen. You're looking very handsome yourself.

Well, there's certainly nothing different about that. But now that you've tapped into your natural beauty, you simply must accompany me to the hospital ball.

I thought you'd never ask. Of course I'll go to the ball with you!

Then we can get married and you can tend to our children as I attempt to save the world one mended bone at a time.

Oh, Stephen, it sounds like a dream come true!

Lucie laughed at something Mann said and touched his arm lightly. Then as she spoke to him she tucked one side of her hair behind her ear and looked up at him from under her pixie lashes.

Holy shit, she was a natural. He'd unleashed a monster.

Reid drained the last half of his beer and tried his damnedest not to march over and drag her home. She shouldn't be flirting with Mann, much less want to have his children. On paper the guy was probably USDA Prime, but Reid couldn't shake the sense that he had hidden flaws that made him no better than Standard Grade.

"I saw you come in with Lucie. You guys seeing each other?" Reid looked over at Eric just as a waiter set down a bucket full of ice and bottlenecks on the table next to them. He smiled and said, "Forethought."

They grabbed their next round, used the bottle opener on the side of the bucket, and tossed their caps. Shaking the excess water off his hand Reid said, "Lucie and I are old friends. I'm staying with her for a bit while I'm in town."

Eric tipped his bottle in Lucie's direction. "Well, the friend thing explains why you're not staking your claim as she flirts with the good doctor over there. But it doesn't quite explain the look in your eye that says you'd like to kill him with your bare hands."

"I fight for a living, so that look is kind of a habit," he answered smoothly.

"Are you also a makeover artist or is our Lucie's

sudden transformation simply a coincidence with your appearance?"

Reid didn't like where the conversation was heading. Eric was too damn observant for his own good. He seemed like a decent guy, though, and he spoke with affection for Lucie. "Have you known Lucie long?"

Eric peered over at where she was still talking with Mann. "I've known her since college." He cut his gaze back to Reid. "She's like a sister to me."

Reid inclined his head in understanding. "Message received, man. I'm her brother's best friend."

A satisfied grin spread over the guy's face and he held up his beer for Reid to tap with his. "Good to hear."

Taking a few generous swallows of his beer, Reid wondered if he could gain any insight about the years he hadn't been around. The ones that very clearly defined who she was as an adult. "Were you around when Lucie got married?"

"Yeah," Eric ground out. "I was around."

"Who was he? What happened?"

"She met him when they literally collided outside of the university one day. She was on her way out of class, and he was involved in some peace rally about whatever his group had their panties in a twist about that week."

Reid knew the exact type Eric described. There were entire groups of them that were constantly speaking out against MMA. They called themselves human activists. He called them uneducated assholes. He tried picturing Lucie with a guy like that and failed. Then again, he couldn't picture her with a guy like Mann either, but clearly she saw something he didn't. "Okay, so the guy was an activist, she was a student, they met. Then what?"

"The relationship was a fricking whirlwind. One day they met for lunch and the next thing we know they're announcing their engagement and eloping to Vegas. The whole thing happened so damn fast it made our heads spin."

"Is that why you didn't like him?"

"Fuck no," Eric snarled. "I *hate* him because of what he did to Lucie. She was so blinded by his passion for saving the world and idealistic dreams that she couldn't see what a total flake he was. That guy couldn't commit to just one entrée in a restaurant much less commit to one woman. He was pretty much just a self-important douchebag who loved attention. "

Reid could see where this was headed and his gut clenched with the familiar desire to put his fists through someone's face. "Tell me what he did," he said through a tight jaw.

Eric tensed and glanced at Lucie. His love for her was evident in the narrowing of his brown eyes as he spoke. "Bastard hooked up with some hippie chick a few months into the marriage. I'd bet a year's salary it wasn't just a one time—or one girl—thing. Anyway, Lucie caught him in the act. In their bed."

Reid swore and had to put his beer down before his grip crushed the bottle. What kind of man does that to such a sweet and innocent woman? Or *any* woman for that matter. It finally made sense why Lucie was so hung up on finding someone she was compatible with. Her ex had been her complete opposite and the relationship had been a joke. Now she needed to find the opposite of that relationship, which was a long courtship to someone as similar to her as possible. Someone, like the guy who was currently whispering in her ear as she laughed. Dr. Stephen Mann, MD.

"Easy, amigo. Your fangs are showing."

Reid cut a glare over to Eric. "What the hell are you talking about?"

"You look like a jungle cat ready to sink your teeth into someone's jugular."

Reid studied the man, wondering why the fuck he was grinning like an idiot. "Is that so?"

"It is. And although I'd love to wheedle the

reason from you, I'll have to be satisfied with my own ruminations."

"Why is that?"

Eric nodded over to the side. "Because Lucie's headed this way." Reid followed his line of sight to see her gliding across the room with the biggest smile he'd ever seen on her. "I've gotta go hit the head. Nice meeting you, Reid. I'll see you around."

"You too, man. Thanks for the beer."

A second later Reid forgot all about Eric's cryptic statements as he focused on Lucie. He felt duplicitous, both wanting to know all the details of her Mann encounter and wanting to pretend like it never happened. But he'd be a pretty shitty friend if he did the latter, so he sucked it up and did the right thing. "So what happened? It looked like you hooked him pretty deep from what I could tell."

Lucie clasped her hands in front of her, seemingly trying not to explode. "It happened just like you said, Reid. He noticed me, said I looked beautiful. Is it hot in here?" She started fanning herself so Reid handed her one of the ridiculous diaper-pin drinks. "Mm, thanks, I'm so thirsty."

A drop of condensation from the glass splashed onto her neck as she tipped her head back to down the entire contents. He had to fist his hands at his sides so he wasn't tempted to wipe it away as it descended to the sexy hollow at the bottom of her throat.

"Anyway," she continued, placing the empty glass on a waiter's tray as he walked by, "we talked for a little while and then he asked me on an actual date. Can you believe it?"

Reid plastered a stiff smile on his face and hoped it passed for the real thing. He had the insane urge to march over there and deck the guy on principle alone. Why the hell wouldn't he have noticed Lucie before the makeover? So her hair was usually a disheveled mess and she wore her glasses instead of contacts and her clothes didn't accentuate the tight little body she possessed. Why had that made her invisible to the doctor for the last several years?

When he'd seen her in her office that first day, he'd liked watching her try to get her errant strands of hair to stay where she wanted them, only to have them fall right after she was done tucking them back. He thought she looked sexy with her glasses on—that whole naughty librarian thing he loved—and she was adorable when she accidentally snorted from laughing too hard or finding something incredulous.

Mann was a vain asshole who didn't deserve Lucie, that's all there was to it. But then again, it's not as if Reid deserved someone like her either. He couldn't offer her what she needed. He didn't live the lifestyle of predictability she craved. When he had fights in other states, other countries, he was more of a nomad than anything. And even if that wasn't an issue, he still could never be with her. Not as he was currently. A loser. A has-been. A wash-up. No, he needed his title and his championship status back if he ever hoped to be worth anything ever again. Nobody loved a loser. His pop had taught him that. Over and over again.

"Reid? Did you hear what I said?"

Blinking a few times he brought her back into focus. "Yeah, I heard you. But I'm not surprised. I told you the guy would be all over you like white on rice."

She gave a tiny little squeal. "I'd totally hug you right now, but you know, he might be watching and I don't want him to get the wrong idea."

"No," he replied wryly. "We wouldn't want that."

His trainer, Butch, was often trying to get Reid to hold back in a fight. "Know when to use restraint," he'd tell him. The point was to keep calm, keep your wits, and let the other guy make the first move so you could defend against it, and then counter with something even stronger. Reid had never been good with the idea of restraint.

He was more comfortable in the position of the aggressor.

He'd always hated those lessons of restraint. But as the night progressed and he was forced to watch Mann circle Lucie like a shark, Reid had to call upon every one of them. By using Butch's mental techniques he managed to keep his distance, thereby allowing Mann to keep his teeth. At least for a little longer.

CHAPTER EIGHT

"Start with the wall stretch."

Reid barely stopped a childish eye roll. "C'mon, Lu, I don't need to do those special stretches anymore. It's been over a week. Let's just get to the normal stuff."

"Oh, I'm sorry, I hadn't realized you had a degree in physical therapy." She turned around once she reached the far wall of her workout-turned-therapy room. "Why did you need my help again?"

"Sarcasm does not become you," he grumbled. But he couldn't be all that grouchy when she looked so good in her new workout clothes. Gone were the oversize tanks and grungy sweats. Now she was sporting a pale pink Lycra tank top with hip-hugging gray yoga pants.

Her dark hair was pulled into a high ponytail

with her thick bangs and some longer pieces framing her face. She'd just finished her morning elliptical routine and her olive skin glistened with sweat and a healthy glow infused her cheeks.

Crossing to where she stood by the paper ruler they'd taped up to track his progress, he became uncharacteristically aware of his own condition from his ten-mile run on the treadmill. He stopped a few feet short and glanced down at his sweat-soaked T-shirt that now looked black as pitch from its previously worn and faded shade.

"What are you doing?" she asked as he stripped it off.

He gave her a crooked smirk. "Trying not to offend your delicate sensibilities."

She snorted and immediately slapped a hand over the lower half of her face. It was obvious she was mortified, but he wasn't sure why. He liked getting that reaction from her. As he closed the few remaining feet, Reid added making her snort more often to his mental list of things to accomplish while staying with her. He loved a challenge.

"Keep your feet about a foot away from the wall and walk your fingers up the ruler until you feel pressure. Then lean in toward the wall until you feel that stretch." He did as instructed, though he'd have rather started with some light lifting to warm up the muscles. This shit was for sissies. "Good. Hold it for about ten seconds…and now back to the starting position."

"This is ridiculous. Can't I get the same result with a five-pound weight in my hand and lifting it in the same manner?"

Her hands planted themselves firmly on her slim hips as she said, "Now why didn't I think of that? Oh, *I* know. Because that wouldn't be stretching the muscles. That would be *working* the muscles."

"Fine, have it your way. But we're combining our training sessions then."

"Wha—"

Her question was cut off with a squeal when his left arm snaked around her waist and pulled her in front of him. "There. Now I have an incentive to lean into the wall."

"Reid, what the hell are you talking about?"

He couldn't help his satisfied grin as he said, "Kissing."

Lucie's eyes went wide and her jaw slackened just enough that her lips barely parted. He waited patiently for the shock to wear off. And for the rebuff he knew was forthcoming.

"Absolutely not. You're out of your damn mind. I'm not kissing you, Andrews."

When he lifted a brow as if to say, *a little late*

for that, she added huffily, "I'm not kissing you *again*."

Shrugging his good shoulder he acted as though he couldn't care less. "You're probably right. I'm sure you know all the little tricks on how to bring a guy to his knees with a simple kiss. Passion obviously comes second nature to you." Then he went in for the kill shot. "Which is why you need *me* to teach you how to get Dr. Mandible in the first place."

He had to be a glutton for epic beatdowns, because that's exactly what he'd get if Jax ever found out Reid kissed his sister. He was extremely protective where she was concerned, and with good reason. It didn't matter that she was only a few years younger than him. She seemed so innocent and naive. Trusting.

So why was it so hard for him to keep his distance around her? Was it because she was the exact opposite of the women he usually dated? Not that he'd "dated" since his injury. When he thought he'd never fight again he'd hit an all-time low, turning down every illicit offer thrown his way. Maybe now that his title shot was within his reach his libido was coming back online finally. Hell, he didn't know what to think anymore.

"Now that you have an actual date with the guy you need to know how to walk the walk,

Luce. You flirted like a champ and hooked him, but if you flake out when it comes time for anything else, you'll give him mixed signals and he'll back out."

She worried her bottom lip as the wheels in her head turned. At last she nodded and the knot in his stomach from the thought of never tasting those lips again unraveled. "Okay. You made your point. Show me what to do."

"First you need to relax. You're wound so tight I'm afraid you'll snap. Turn around."

Holding her shoulders, he turned her until her back was to him, and then began massaging her upper back and shoulders. Instantly she melted into his hands on a moan. "I can't remember the last time someone gave me a massage. That feels so fantastic."

"That's a shame," he said, studying the curve of her neck as her head fell forward. "Everyone should have someone to rub the day's stress away."

"Mmm," she said in way of agreeing. "Who does that for you?"

A parade of random women who'd been more than happy to give him a thorough rubdown as a prelude to sex marched through his mind. For some reason, being here with Lucie, the whole scene seemed…less enticing. "Like all athletes, we have sports medicine people at the gym who do that for us."

"Mmm."

He smiled, loving the simple pleasure he was giving her with his hands. He pushed his thumbs up the centerline of her neck to the base of her skull, then massaged in tiny outward circles. She took in a slow, deep breath and let it out on a breathy moan as her shoulders pulled down in a relaxing stretch.

"Good." Reid moved his hands to her shoulders and worked on the knots between her shoulder blades. Before he could stop himself he leaned in, placing his face on the side of her head. Her hair tickled his cheek, and its flowery scent, paired with the anticipation of tasting her again, made his mouth water.

He turned his head ever so slightly to speak in her ear. "Keep this feeling of relaxation and carelessness. Stay out of your head, okay?"

She nodded and he turned her around so her back was against the wall once again. With his right arm, he began walking his fingers up the wall for the stretch, bringing him closer to her with every inch he gained. Talk about incentive.

"Right now your focus is on my eyes…"

"Uh-huh…"

"But if you're looking to get kissed, where

should your eyes be?"

Her gaze drifted lower and settled heavily on his mouth. The pale gray of her eyes changed to a molten silver. Her lashes weren't the impossibly thick and long kind he was used to seeing, but then again, it'd been a long time since he'd seen a girl scrubbed free of makeup, much less without fake eyelashes. He rather liked Lucie's. They were thick at the lash line, but then gathered together to form triangular spikes that curved up only slightly. Just how he imagined a pixie's lashes would be.

She swept the tip of her tongue over her lips, making them glisten with moisture. Only a few inches separated them now as his right hand was as high as it could go without causing pain. Now to lean into the stretch.

As he slowly, slowly closed the space between them, he heard her breaths turn to pants and his own heart beat double-time against his ribs. When their lips barely touched, their breaths mingling, he paused, giving her the opportunity to take the lead. To take what she wanted.

She didn't.

At the end of the ten seconds, he walked his hand back down the wall until he was standing straight again, arm by his side.

Reid studied her for a minute, trying to figure

out how to get her to act rather than think. Again he walked his hand up the wall, drawing closer to her as he spoke. "Tell me what you want."

"I don't understand."

"There's a reason we're doing this. You want something. Don't think about the answer. I want you to *feel* the answer. Now," he said once he'd gone as far as he could and began to lean toward her, "tell me, what you want."

She licked her lips. Swallowed hard as his mouth got closer, but stayed just out of reach. "Right now?"

"Right this very instant."

"I want to kiss you so badly it scares me."

Her answer shocked the hell out of him—he'd been expecting her to say something along the lines of wanting her doctor—but he was too selfish to give a damn.

"Then do something about it," he commanded.

Lucie grabbed the sides of his face and meshed her mouth on his. This time, saltiness left behind from her workout mixed with the strawberry taste of her lips. The combination was intoxicating, but it was nothing compared to the one-two punch he got when she swept her tongue over his upper lip.

Reid took that as an open invitation. Plunging his tongue inside her mouth was like tasting sweet ambrosia.

He hoped like hell his boxer briefs would do a better job of containing his growing erection than he did of containing the toe-curling groan that escaped his chest.

She pulled away, switching immediately into therapist mode. Although she wasn't usually so breathless when assessing him. He liked her affected like this. A lot. "This isn't a good idea, Reid. You need to stay focused with the stretches or you'll cause yourself more pain."

With his left hand on her chin, he dragged her attention away from his injury. "My shoulder isn't in pain right now, Lu. However, I can't say the same for another place of my anatomy."

He waited patiently for her innocent mind to catch up with his fiendish one wallowing in the gutter. To no avail. "I don't understand, where are you in pain?"

He hitched his left brow and quirked up a corner of his mouth in the universal smirk that said, "I'm thinkin' dirty." Now she'd get it in three…two…one…

A slight widening of those light gray eyes and a sudden interest in the ceiling above his head told him he was right on the money. He would've laughed at how charming he found the blush in her cheeks, but he wasn't exactly in the laughing mood. Nope. His mind had already hopped onto the one track that was headed straight for trouble. The fun kind.

"I know I'm not your type, Reid. You don't have to make things up to make me feel better about myself. I'm a big girl."

Was she fucking serious? She didn't think he was turned on by her? Now *that* was enough to piss him right the hell off. Abandoning the stupid stretch, he grabbed her ass in both hands and pulled her into his body.

Hard.

This time she gasped and planted her hands on his pecs in a feeble attempt to keep some semblance of space in the equation. Lucky for him, that wasn't the half he was concerned with obliterating everything between them but their clothes. And even those weren't a safe bet at this point. To prove it, he ground his pelvis forward, letting the hard length of his cock rub against the nerve-sensitive juncture between her legs.

"Feel that, Lucie? That's not how I react to women I'm not into. Believe me, there are other ways of teaching you these things. Less intimate ways." Ways that he should damn well be using. But instead he trailed one of his hands up her side and swept his thumb over her nipple, eliciting a wanton moan from her kiss-swollen lips. Even through the material of her sports bra and tank top he could see her nipple pucker and harden from his touch. He hissed in appreciation. "I just can't seem to leave myself out of this."

"Why not?" she said with just a hint of trembling.

Why not? That was the million-dollar question, wasn't it? Why *couldn't* he step back from her? Why was it that every time he pictured her doing anything with another guy, much less that asshole of a doctor she was so hung up on, his gut clenched like he'd just been sucker punched by a heavyweight?

"I don't know," he answered honestly. "All I know is I'm tired of fighting myself when I'm near you like this. So maybe I shouldn't. Maybe starting right now we come up with a new plan."

He wasn't sure if she realized it or not, but Lucie's hands left his chest and slid up behind his neck, allowing her breasts to mold themselves against him. Damn, he loved the way her softness gave way to his harder body.

"What are you suggesting?"

He dipped his head until they were so close they were sharing breaths, their noses lightly brushing as they danced around their overwhelming desire to fuse their mouths. "Maybe the best way to teach you how to seduce, is to let you feel what it's like to *be* seduced. And then let you try it out on someone who's not your eventual target. So you get any nerves out of the way."

"Like a trial run."

"Right. In the end I go back to reclaim my title like I want, and you bag what's-his-nuts, just like you want. No strings, no hard feelings. But in the meantime, we blow off some steam and get whatever the hell this is out of our systems."

"I suppose that makes sense. It's definitely a plan with merits." Her long fingers at his nape slipped up into the hair at the base of his skull as she tipped her head back, exposing the smooth expanse of her neck for his nibbling pleasure. "Oh, God." The prayer was a breathy whisper, just barely loud enough for him to hear, and made him grin with base satisfaction as he moved up to the space just behind her ear. She tasted like salted caramel, a combination it seemed he couldn't get enough of.

"So what do you say, Luce?" He nipped at her earlobe and then soothed it with a gentle suction in his mouth.

"I say—" Her answer was cut off by a gasp as he pushed her back the few inches to press her up against the wall.

"You were saying?" Reid prompted her to

start her sentence again, knowing damn well he wasn't going to let her finish. It was too much fun interrupting her.

"I was saying that— *uhn*!" That time he ground himself over where he knew that sensitive little bundle was swollen and aching for some contact. "Damn it, Reid, yes, okay? I say yes to the new plan!"

"About damn time you spit that out." And with that, he attacked.

CHAPTER NINE

Lucie felt like she just sold her soul to the devil, and she couldn't care less. In all her life she'd never felt so wanted, so desired. Reid was setting her on fire and she was more than happy to go down in flames.

The air surrounding them was humid with an eclectic array of scents. Sweat, both old and new, carried undertones of her jasmine shampoo and something of his that reminded her of ocean foam and sunshine.

He buried his face in her neck. She had no idea so many wonderful things could be done to one's neck. Kissing, suckling, biting, licking. Each was more erotic than the last and took with it another fraction of her sanity.

The man moved like he'd been training to do *this* his whole life instead of fight. She certainly never experienced anything close to this with her ex-husband. Reid consumed her with what should logically be considered basic moves, and all she could think to do was wrap her arms around his shoulders, dig her fingers into his strong back, and hold on for dear life.

With one hand he grabbed her thigh and held it on his hip as he performed another of those magical pelvic thrusts. The new position opened her up, allowing the hard length of him to cause delicious friction at her very center. Suddenly she wished their clothing would spontaneously combust. There were way too many barriers between them.

"I want inside of you so damn bad," he breathed against her jaw. "I can't remember the last time I was this hard."

"That's a good thing, though, right?"

He pulled back just enough to look down at her as he answered. And lucky her, it also provided him with room to trace, pluck, and torture a nipple with his free hand, eliciting an *Oh, God* and a few accompanying moans. "Good *and* bad. Good, because it means I'm extremely turned on by you. Bad, because it means I'm going to embarrass the hell out of myself when I don't last longer than a few minutes."

"Really?" Lucie tried to remember the act

of sex ever lasting more than a few minutes and came up blank. She'd sort of assumed that was the norm, but she wasn't telling *him* that. Trying to look nonchalant, she asked, "So, how long would you say is your average?"

Reid laughed as he hoisted her up with her legs around his waist and his weight pressing her into the wall. She was almost at eye level with him now, making it impossible not to be transfixed by the amusement dancing in his mossy-brown irises. "I think that's the male equivalent of asking a woman her weight. But it doesn't matter because I think, with a little practice, we're going to leave my average in the dust."

That didn't really tell her much, but it sounded promising. Only, he didn't give her a chance to ponder it for more than a second before he took her mouth in a heated kiss. His tongue delved between her lips and massaged hers. He tasted faintly of an Andes chocolate mint, which was likely from his toothpaste and protein shake, but made her want to suck on him until he melted in her mouth.

With his hips holding her up against the wall, his hands were free to roam. As he continued his plundering kiss, the fingers of one hand traced the crease of her ass and down to stroke her swollen folds, while the other worked under her shirt and pushed up one side of her bra to gain access to a taut breast.

Her mind was wrapped in cotton, unable to conjure the simplest of thoughts. Her only possible function right now was to focus on every stroke, every touch, and await the moment when he would finally sink inside her. The image made her sex clench, but there was nothing to hold onto. She was empty, achingly so, and it made her whimper with need and squeeze his waist in frustration.

"I know, baby. I know what you need. Whaddya say we take this into your bedroom so I can satisfy you right?"

It should've been a question. It was posed as one. But it wasn't asked like one. There was no need for it to be. No woman in her right mind would have said no. But just as he held her to him and turned to walk from the room, they heard the front door slam shut and Reid froze mid-turn.

"Lucie? Where are ya, girl?"

Her eyes stretched wide and she muttered "Macaroni Matinee!" behind the hand now covering her mouth.

Reid mouthed *What?* but there was no time to explain. The apartment wasn't that big, and it wouldn't be long before Vanessa found her in a very compromising position. Lucie put weight into her legs, forcing him to put her down, but her legs were about as steady as cooked pasta, and she was forced to sink onto the weight bench behind her.

While trying to adjust her bra and tank top she called out to her best friend. "I'm in the workout room, Nessie! Can you grab me a bottle of water from the fridge?" That should buy them a few extra seconds. Once she was sure she was sufficiently put together, Lucie breathed a sigh of relief.

Then she looked at Reid and had a mini-panic attack.

Was he even wearing underwear? His shorts were tented like Barnum & Bailey's big top. Snatching his discarded shirt at her feet she threw it at him and whispered, "Quick! Put it on."

When all he did was quirk a brow in her direction she very pointedly looked at his crotch. After glancing down and probably realizing he couldn't see the floor between his feet, he caught on and pulled it over his head just as Vanessa was rounding the corner.

"I know I'm a little early, but— *Whoa.*" Vanessa stopped in the doorway, a water bottle in one hand and a Diet Mountain Dew in the other from the stockpile Lucie kept on hand specifically for her addict of a friend. "Who's your guest?" Before Lucie had the opportunity to make the introductions, Vanessa moved forward, handed off the bottle of water without sparing a glance in her direction, and extended her hand. "Hi, I'm Vanessa MacGregor. And you are?"

Reid responded with a handshake and one of his killer smiles. "Reid Andrews."

"Very nice to meet you, Reid. You'll have to forgive me for being so surprised, but I didn't realize Lucie had company."

Lucie cracked open the bottle of water and drank nearly its entire contents in one shot. She loved Vanessa like a sister and had never once been jealous of the attention her friend garnered everywhere they went. Until now. No doubt Reid was undressing her in his mind this very moment. She was stunningly beautiful from her tight, curly strawberry hair to her legs-up-to-her-neck model figure. Lucie didn't think of herself as ugly by any means, but she was mature enough to be comfortable with her "unremarkable" features. Everything about her was just sort of…well, ordinary.

She'd watched countless men at Fritz's hang on Vanessa's every word and drool over every sway of her hips. It was practically a spectator sport on dart league nights and Vanessa never reacted to any of it. Lucie wasn't sure if she was just that oblivious or just that modest.

She doubted it was the former since she had the reputation of being one of the shrewdest attorneys in the area. Plus, to even be considered *potential* dating material with Vanessa, a man had to pass a whole battery of tests. It was socially acceptable to sell used cars to the public if they passed checklists a fraction the size of Vanessa's. Lucie didn't think there was a man alive who could pass them all yet.

"He's a patient of mine, Ness."

"Ah," Vanessa said with a wink and a smile, "then in this case I can see why you'd want to bring your work home with you."

Reid chuckled in a too-adorable flattered manner as he crossed his arms over his chest, stretching the cotton over his shoulders and biceps. "Actually, I've known Lucie most of my life; I'm best friends with her brother."

"Oh, you're from Sun Valley! That's great; I've never met anyone from before Lucie and I were roomies as freshmen. I hope you'll share some embarrassing stories I can use for ammo. The girl has an entire blackmail portfolio on me, and I've got absolutely nothing on her. It's seriously unfair."

"Sorry, Ness, but I've told you before there are no skeletons in my closet. I was just as boring before college as I am now."

"And I've told *you* before, you're not boring. You're conservative to my crazy, which is why we're so good together. We balance each other out." Vanessa popped the top of her soda and held her can out toward Lucie who then touched her water bottle to it before they said, "Salut," and drank.

Vanessa walked the few feet to sit next to Lucie on the weight bench. "So are you done with your session? You have to hurry up and get ready if we're going to make our Macaroni Matinee."

"Oh, um…" Crap, her throat was dry. Why did nerves make her throat so damn dry? It was such a ridiculous physiological reaction. She stalled while taking another swig of water.

"What's a Macaroni Matinee? Sounds like the lunch special at a senior center."

Vanessa barked out a laugh as Lucie almost spit out the water in her mouth and then sputtered a second before she could safely swallow. Thankfully Vanessa answered so she could finish coughing in peace. "It's our monthly girl date. The first Saturday of every month we see a movie and eat lunch at the Macaroni Grill and gorge ourselves on heart-attack-sized portions of carbs."

"Ness, I can't go for a while."

"What?" Somehow she managed to make

those gorgeous green eyes grow twice as big. Whenever Vanessa wanted something, she had a way of looking like Puss in Boots from *Shrek* when he used his pathetic kitty face. "But I've had a really shitty week in court and I need some major girl time where we do nothing but make horrible, judgy comments about other women and scope out guys' asses in tight jeans."

"But I can't just leave Reid…" Lucie looked over at him with a look that said, *Forgive me for what I'm about to suggest, but I don't know what to do here.* "Unless, you want to come with us?"

He laughed and held out his hands in resignation. "That's okay, Lu. As much as I'd love the opportunity to scope out other guys' asses, I'll have to pass. Unfortunately, I can't afford the carb overload right now. And speaking of that, I need to do some more grocery shopping for the house. Is there anything specific you want me to get?"

"No, what you picked up last week was great. It's going to be hard to get used to my pathetic microwave dinners again after you're gone. Who knew healthly food could be so tasty?"

"Whoa! I need a recess here."

"This isn't a courtroom, Nessie."

"Are you *living* here?"

Lucie spoke quickly to keep any required damage control to a minimum. "Just for a couple of months until he's recovered from his torn rotator cuff. I've taken my vacation weeks to work with Reid on a vigorous recovery and training program."

"Wow, Luce, that's really something else. I'm speechless."

No you're not, but you're holding your tongue—albeit only temporarily—and I love you for it. "Well, I suppose I'd better get ready then."

"Yeah, get a move on. You know how I hate getting bad seats in the theater." Vanessa got up and crossed the room, adding, "I'll be in the living room thumbing through your latest issue of Boring Medical Magazine hoping there's a piece on the male gluteus maximus, complete with pictures."

Once they heard her plop on the couch and set her soda on the table they looked at each other and quietly laughed in relief.

"She's a trip," he said.

Lucie stood, grateful her legs worked again. "You have *no* idea."

"She's very protective of you. She didn't like it when you called yourself boring." He took a step toward her, the playfulness gone. "Neither did I, by the way."

"It's the truth, though. I've never done anything wild or crazy or, God forbid, illegal." She shrugged and picked imaginary lint from her new pants. "I'm a rule player."

Another step. Now he was so close she could feel his breath on her skin. Lucie glanced at the doorway. What if Vanessa decided to walk back in? Fingers to her chin brought her attention up to him. "The only time I follow the rules is in the cage," he said in a low voice.

"That mentality can get you into a lot of trouble."

"I happen to like trouble." His lopsided grin was so wicked. And delectable. Which was a weird way to describe a grin, but there it was. She wanted to lick it from one side to the other. "Go get ready and enjoy your girl outing. I'll finish my stretches and exercises after I go to the store. Then later…" He dropped his gaze to her mouth and trailed a thumb over her lower lip. "…we'll finish the other thing we started."

"You still want to?" Lucie barely prevented herself from clapping a hand over her mouth. Sometimes she swore her ability to keep her internal monologues *internal* was faulty. It seemed she was forever trying to extract her size nine from her mouth.

His eyes narrowed slightly. "Don't you?"

Shit. Was he asking because he hoped she still wanted to or because he hoped she didn't, giving him the opportunity to bow out gracefully? And why did she insist on always overthinking these things? *Because you're in way over your head with this one, girlie.*

"Yes?" A single brow arched, challenging her to take the damn question mark off her answer. "Yes. I mean yes." She sighed in exasperation and wished for the thousandth time for the grace and calm Vanessa had. "I thought maybe you were just caught up in the heat of the moment, but now that you've had time to think, maybe you have second thoughts about getting involved."

When his brows pulled together, she quickly added, "Not *involved* involved. I mean, I know it's only temporary and solely for instructional purposes."

Reid moved so fast she didn't have time to register his intentions before she found herself drowning in the heat of his mouth, his tongue lashing and coaxing. Her body was pressed to his with one hand in the center of her back, and his other hand—holy *God*, his other hand—was tucked between her thighs, his fingers pushing between her folds as his thumb worked over her clit. The material of her pants only heightened the friction, and the sense that they couldn't take things too far for fear of being caught was exciting.

It was a fierce and risky move, but he didn't hesitate to execute it to the fullest extent, just like the kind of thing he did in his fights. It's what she loved most about his style in the cage.

The trembling deep in her belly tightened and spread out in ripples. As the sensations mounted she dug her fingers into his triceps to anchor herself for the coming tidal wave. He broke the kiss causing a whine of protest to fall from her lips, and when his fingers stopped their magical caresses, her pelvis automatically tried following them to beg for more as they retreated.

"Did that put your concerns about me reconsidering to rest?" She nodded. "Good. Then we'll continue this later."

Her fingers automatically contracted when she felt him start to pull away. "Please, Reid. I'm so close," she whispered. Lucie hadn't climaxed in so long she wondered if she even remembered what it felt like. She used to take care of things herself, but after months of long hours at the office and falling into bed exhausted at night, she lost the energy to even bother. She was probably considered asexual by now. At the ripe, old age of twenty-nine and a quarter.

"I know, but I won't give it to you right now. And it has nothing to do with Vanessa in the next room, because believe me, if I wanted to, I'd take

you up against that wall and not give a damn if
she watched while eating popcorn like it was one
of your movie dates."

"Then why?" Oh, God, was she actually *whining*?

He held the side of her face as he spoke, his
intense eyes doing nothing to help cool her down.
"Because when I make you come for the first
time I don't want you holding back. I want to hear
every hitch of your breath." He placed a kiss at
her temple. "Every moan." Another kiss on her
cheek. "And I won't be satisfied until you scream
my name."

She would have groaned in frustration, but
the kiss he gave her swallowed any sound that
dared escape. After several heady moments he
pulled away and gave her a devilish smile. "If it
makes you feel better, there's a lesson in this."

"I'm fairly certain I hate this lesson," she said
in a breathy voice between large gulps of air.

"Lesson number three: always leave them
wanting more." He chuckled—he actually had the
audacity to find that funny—and nipped her lip,
then soothed it with the tip of his tongue. "Have
fun today."

Incredulous, Lucie watched Reid disappear
from the room then heard him say good-bye to
Vanessa before heading to the bathroom for a
shower. Yep. She definitely hated this lesson.

CHAPTER TEN

"Two usuals, Fritz!" Vanessa called down to the old, grizzled man at the other end of the bar.

"Don't get yer panties in a twist, Red, I'll get to ya in a minute!"

"I'd have to be *wearing* panties to keep them out of a twist."

"Well, that's better than that ass floss these broads wear nowadays."

"How would *you* know what broads are wearing? The last action you probably saw was World War II, geezer."

"Ha! I got stories that would make yer hair even curlier than it is now, missy, an' don't you ferget it."

Lucie laughed at the typical back and forth between Vanessa and the owner of the bar they'd been coming to since college. Fritz was more like a lovable uncle to them, but that didn't mean their humor with each other didn't cross into faux flirtation and dirty jokes. He was the quintessential dirty old man, and they adored him.

After Fritz served them their tap beers in large glass steins, he kissed the fingers of both his hands and placed one on each of their cheeks. "There. Now shut yer yaps and go kick some ass tonight, huh?"

"Will do, Fritzy," Vanessa pledged before they made their way to the other end of the bar by the dartboards. They claimed their usual stools and clinked their glasses together with an enthusiastic "Salut" and took their first glorious sips. Nessie slapped a hand on the bar three times, which was her way of gaveling for an audience. "Spill."

Lucie hitched her eyebrows under her bangs and looked at her beer. "I'd rather drink it if it's all the same to you." She might be a lightweight when it came to wine, but she could hang pretty well with beer from years of practice with Vanessa since their college days.

"I'm not encouraging alcohol abuse. I'm telling you to tell me what's up with you and the hottie staying in your apartment. I waited patiently all during lunch for you to bring him up, but you were sadly close-mouthed about your new houseguest. So prepare for the witness stand."

For the second time that day Lucie choked on her drink. *Oh, for shit's sake. You'd better learn to control yourself or eventually you're going to need the Heimlich if you dare to eat again.* "No need for cross-examination or whatever, Nessie. Nothing's up with him. He's Jackson's best friend, and I'm helping him out, that's all."

"Is he seeing anyone?"

"No." Wait a minute. She didn't really know that for sure, did she? He hadn't mentioned dating anyone, but she hadn't really asked either. There hadn't been any reason to. They were just two friends who were helping each other. But the definition of "helping" had changed drastically in the course of a week. "At least, I don't think he is. But he's not your type anyway."

"I wasn't planning on pursuing him, but out of curiosity, why not?"

"Rule number three."

"Really? What does he do then?"

"He's a fighter like Jackson."

Vanessa scrunched up her nose like someone had just shoved smelly socks in her face. "Oh, one of *those* guys. God, how barbaric, not to mention completely irresponsible for planning one's future. No thank you."

Lucie didn't bother defending Reid's and her

brother's choice of career to her friend. There'd be no point. Vanessa lived by a very strict code of rules and refused to veer from them for any reason. She'd gotten the idea one night when they were just freshmen, drunk, and watching the television drama, *NCIS*. The main character of the show had over thirty rules he lived by, and Vanessa, in all her inebriated wisdom, decided she needed the same strategy to avoid following in her parents' dysfunctional footsteps. Rule number three was "never date a man who isn't gainfully employed in a successful career with longevity." Athletes with the potential to permanently injure themselves at a young age, effectively ending their careers, did not qualify as dating potential.

"But why don't *you* date him? I mean, come on, the man is a total hunk of man-beef."

"Ew!" Both girls fell into a fit of laughter. The alcohol was already loosening them up from their long weeks. "What the hell is man-beef? Stick to legal jargon because you obviously suck at complimentary descriptions."

"Don't avoid the question. What about dating him?"

"No."

"Why not?"

"It's not like that."

"But it could be."

"Just drop it, okay, Ness?"

Vanessa's dark lashes practically twined together as she dissected Lucie's face. *Shit shit shit.* "What aren't you telling me, Lucinda Maris?"

It always touched Lucie when her friend refused to call her by her married name. She'd told Lucie she should "sever every tie she had to that bastard," but she hadn't wanted to. She needed it as a reminder to guard her heart more carefully. Relationships based on a foundation of heady passion and quick courtships were doomed for failure. What she needed was the exact opposite: a foundation of mutual interests and goals, complemented by mild attraction, and at least two years of dating followed by a long engagement.

She drank half of her beer in several big gulps and then placed the glass on the bar with a resigned sigh. Once Vanessa suspected she wasn't being told "the truth, the whole truth, and nothing but the truth" she was like a pit bull. "Reid needs to complete his recovery and get ready to fight for this big rematch he has in two months."

"And?"

"And I agreed to take my vacation weeks to give him special around-the-clock attention to make sure he could fight if he did something for me."

"And that something would beeeeeee…"

Lucie looked around as she bit the inside of her cheek before finally leaning in to make sure her friend was the only one who could hear her. "That he teach me how to seduce Stephen."

"*What!*"

"Shhhhhh! Keep your voice down, you nutbag."

"*I'm* the nutbag? Luce, when are you going to realize that that guy does *not* deserve you? Is that the reason for your new wardrobe? I mean, you look fabulous, but if that douchebag didn't notice you before the clothes and these *lessons,* then it's his fucking loss."

"Yeah, I know, you've mentioned something like that before once or twice," Lucie replied wryly. The truth of the matter was Vanessa hadn't approved of her crush on the good doctor when he failed to make a move after they'd worked together a year. "Look, can we not talk about this anymore? It's harshing my buzz."

"Mine too. Okay, it's officially off the table for tonight. Kyle and Eric just walked in, so I'll get us more beer before we start. Save my spot."

Lucie threw her legs up onto Vanessa's vacated stool and waved to the other half of their team. At least the guys would act as a buffer from the whole Reid-Stephen issue. She'd been on a rollercoaster ever since Stephen walked into her

office last Friday morning, followed promptly by
Reid's surprise visit and even more surprising
offer.

The heavy make-out session had only served
to teach her what it felt like to be rode hard and
put up wet. And she hadn't even been able to
enjoy her lunch and movie with Vanessa because
she'd been anticipating the grilling she knew was
coming. Now that it was out of the way, though,
she fully intended to enjoy the next couple hours
of drama-free fun. She'd texted Reid earlier and
apologized for forgetting about league night and
told him not to wait up for her since she knew he
went to bed fairly early with the strict training
schedule he kept.

When the realization hit her that she wouldn't
see Reid until tomorrow morning, Lucie downed
the rest of her beer and eased further into her
stool. Yep. Nothing to worry about, nothing to
be anxious about. Just a couple of carefree dart
games and drinks with her friends. She so needed
this.

• • •

Reid walked into the dive bar that Vanessa had
suggested he come to as he'd been on his way out
earlier that day. He hadn't planned on going, but

when Lucie texted to say he shouldn't wait up for her, he knew she was avoiding him and what he promised her would happen when she got home that night. It shouldn't have bothered him. But it did. And he didn't have a clue as to why.

What he did know was that as he'd shopped for groceries that afternoon he tried to think of more meals Lucie might like. And that train of thought inevitably led to images of teaching her how to cook said meals, complete with letting her taste things from his finger…and then from his tongue. And *that* led to him looking like he was smuggling a cucumber in his shorts as he strolled through the produce section.

Standing by the door he scanned the room for Vanessa, figuring she'd be the easiest to spot with her height and wild red hair. Two seconds later his sweep was brought to an abrupt halt. Damn, had he been wrong.

She stood in a group that was clearly the dart league she was a part of. He recognized Vanessa and Eric, but even they sort of blurred out once his eyes found Lucie. She wore a phenomenal pair of dark jean capris that hugged her ass and sat low on her slim hips, paired with a pale orange baby tee with the classic Crush soda logo emblazoned on the front. He'd liked how the logo curved around her breasts when she'd tried it on in the store. Now he was kicking himself for adding it to her wardrobe since every other guy in the bar probably liked it for the same fucking reason.

She looked so different from how he'd seen her the last week. Not only in her appearance, but also her spirit. She had an inner glow shining through. He stood back, content to watch her in her element for a while. Her smile was so big that for the first time he noticed a small dimple in her right cheek. Her long chestnut hair was pulled back in some sort of a haphazard bun that looked to be held in place with stir sticks from the bar. She cheered on Vanessa who was throwing darts at the closest dartboard of three to where she and two guys were standing. When Vanessa's last dart hit the board, all four started cheering. The blond guy next to Lucie picked her up by the waist and spun her around before giving her a big smack on the lips.

And she didn't even flinch.

Knowing his reaction was unfounded, if not downright ludicrous, Reid stalked across the room, using his height and broad shoulders to his advantage to push through the rowdy bar patrons. Lucie didn't see his approach as she was facing away from him, but Vanessa beamed a radiant smile when she noticed him standing behind

Lucie.

"Hiya, Reid! I'm so glad you decided to come! You're just in time to celebrate our first victory of the night."

Lucie didn't turn around for a good five seconds, maybe longer. But as soon as Vanessa had said his name, a noticeable tension straightened her spine. When at last she faced him, her smile reached no further than the slight curve of her lips. She wasn't happy to see him. No doubt because he was interrupting the fun with her new admirer. "Reid. What are you doing here?"

"I invited him before we went out this afternoon," Vanessa said. "I thought he could join us for a few drinks, or at least watch us indulge if it went against his überstrict diet or whatever."

He leaned down and lowered his voice so that only she could hear. "I had this crazy notion that maybe you were avoiding me because you were nervous about tonight. But it looks more like you didn't want me cock blocking you with Blondie over there."

As he straightened, his own words burned him like acid pouring over his eardrums. What a dick thing to say to her. She didn't deserve that, and the look of hurt and confusion on her face did him in. Grabbing her hand he led her through the room to the alcove where a pay phone hung on the wall.

"Fuck, I'm sorry, Lu. I acted like a prick. If you're about to get lucky or whatever with that guy, then that's…" He brushed a hand over his hair from back to front and then dragged it over the stubble on his cheeks. "Then that's great," he finally forced out.

"Reid, that's really sweet of you—I think—but what are you talking about? There's no guy I'm about to get lucky with here."

He pointed in the direction of where he'd seen them together. "I saw him kiss you, Lucie, and you didn't exactly look surprised when he did it."

"That's because he does it all the time."

She said that like it should've been all the explanation he needed. But the situation made even less sense now.

"Come on." Now it was her turn to grab his hand and lead them back to where they'd started from. She gestured to the blond dude who'd had his lips all over his girl. Hold up, what? *Lucie*. He'd had his lips all over *Lucie*. "Reid, I'd like you to meet Kyle. Kyle, this is Jackson's best friend and my patient slash house guest slash…um, personal trainer."

From the corner of his eye he saw an impish

grin steal over her face, which was sexy as hell. She was obviously proud of her play on words with their unique relationship, and he had to admit, it was pretty damn clever. Kyle held out his hand and Reid shook it like a good sport, but he made sure to add a little extra pressure and a meaningful stare in the universal male Don't-fuck-with-this-chick-or-I'll-eat-your-heart-for-breakfast-with-my-Wheaties look.

The guy wasn't a slouch in the muscle department, but it made no difference. With Reid's training he could take any street fighter, no matter their size, if it came down to that.

"And you already met Eric last night," she added.

Reid turned and shook Eric's hand. "Eric. Didn't think I'd see you so soon."

"Lucky for me," Eric said with a smile. "Now you can buy my beers tonight."

Lucie interjected with a pointed look at Reid. "Kyle is Eric's *partner*."

"At the hospital?"

Kyle smiled behind his beer as he took a drink and Eric laughed as he answered, "No, man, you missed it. Lucie emphasized the word 'partner.' She all but did the air quotes with her fingers for you."

"Air quotes?"

Vanessa was actually doubled over with laughter, but thankfully took a break to help him out. "They're lovers, Reid. Eric and Kyle are gay."

Reid cut a look over to Lucie for confirmation. Shit. Well, didn't this just change everything. Holding his hand out to Kyle again, he said, "I'm sorry, bro. I just assumed…"

"That I was macking on Lucie? Don't sweat it, man, I totally get it. You were just standing in for Jackson as a protective brother. But you've got a better chance of me hitting on you than our adorable Lucie here."

Eric narrowed his eyes at his partner and Reid couldn't resist a little tit for tat.

"Careful, amigo," Reid said. "Your fangs are showing."

"Yeah, I know. Kyle thinks it's fun to see my hackles go up." Then he turned to Kyle who seemed to be rather enjoying the exchange with his arms crossed over his chest. "Watch yourself, K, or you'll pay for it later. That's a promise."

Kyle just scoffed, not the least bit intimidated by the threat. "You should know by now that I don't do things by accident. I'll go get us another round." Before Eric had the chance for a retort Kyle winked at Reid—not the flirtatious kind, but the kind that said he was having fun pissing off his partner—and then walked past him to the bar.

"Hey, Orange Crush!" The five of them turned in the direction of the guy yelling over the crowd, but it was clear as to who he was addressing. Reid decided he was hiding that damn shirt when they got home. "You're up!"

"Oh, crap, game three started," Lucie said before finishing off the last few swallows of beer. "We lost the first game and won the second, so whichever team wins this one goes to the playoffs. Wish me luck!"

Her teammates all raised their glasses and yelled, "Luck!" at the same time. It seemed to be something they probably did often. Now that he was no longer seeing red, it was obvious they were a tight-knit group.

Reid bought a bottle of water and settled in to watch Lucie play darts. Every time she was done throwing she'd stand next to him at the bar as they all talked and laughed. He'd tried offering her the stool he was on, but she declined saying that she'd just be getting up every few minutes or so anyway. It seemed like most of the players didn't bother sitting down, choosing to stand on the perimeter of their respective dart board and cheer on their friends and try to distract their opponents.

That was fine with him because sitting sideways as he was with the bar to his right and the dartboards to his left, Lucie just happened to stand casually between his knees. And since her friends stood just beyond her, it gave Reid the perfect opportunity to touch her without anyone being the wiser.

The first time he did anything—a light caress over her lower back with one finger—she actually flinched in surprise. Because someone had recently put a heck of a lot of quarters in the jukebox, everyone had to either shout over the raucous music or speak directly into a person's ear. Yet another thing working in his favor. Placing his lips to Lucie's ear he said, "Easy, baby. No one can see that I'm touching you. Take your hair down, Luce. I like it down."

After a fortifying drink of her beer she reached up with one hand and pulled the plastic rods from her hair, placing them on the bar. Her thick hair cascaded to her shoulder blades in the back with shorter pieces in the front to frame her face. She had Pantene-commercial hair, but she rarely wore it down, which was a shame.

The next time she came back from her turn, she once again situated herself between his legs and started talking to Eric and Kyle as Vanessa took her spot at the dartboard. As she listened to Kyle tell a story of some event from work and responded appropriately at all the right times,

Reid slid a hand up the back of her shirt, being careful to stay close to her so no one could see what he was doing. He wanted to make her hyperaware of him, not give the whole bar a show.

Gently he caressed her, dragging his fingers down the dip of her spine, trailing his thumb across her waistline under the edge of her jeans. Below the bar, her hand that had been resting on his knee now clenched, digging short nails into the denim of his pants.

Without missing a beat he answered a question from Kyle as Vanessa returned and Eric now left. Holding her hips he discreetly pulled her back the last few inches so she could feel exactly where his thoughts were. A shiver went through her body when they made contact, and it sure as hell wasn't because it was cold in the stuffy bar.

"Come on, Eric, you can do this!" Vanessa shouted. "Just one more to go. All you need is a triple eighteen and we're in the playoffs, baby!"

Reid bent his head close to her ear. "Do you usually stay and celebrate after the games are over?" She nodded. "Tonight I want you to tell them you're tired, sick, getting abducted by aliens, whatever you want. You're coming back with me."

She turned in his arms and leaned in to answer. "Vanessa will know something's up if I don't get a ride back with her. And she won't let this whole thing with you go enough as it is."

He inclined his head and stood. "Fine. I'll be waiting for you. Don't be long, Lucie. I find I'm not a very patient man at the moment."

Reid said his good-byes, gave Lucie one last meaningful look, and strode out of the bar into the heavy night air. He'd give her thirty minutes. Tops.

CHAPTER ELEVEN

Lucie faced the door of her apartment, studying every nuance of the tarnished brass 3C and the peephole below it…and stalling like a virgin on prom night for going on five minutes now.

She didn't know why she was so nervous in the first place. She certainly had no nerves when Reid was touching her. No, then it was pure fire, unbridled desire like she'd never known. So all she had to do was make it into Reid's arms, and she'd be fine.

She turned the doorknob and entered her apartment. The small lamp with a burgundy shade on the console table by the door cast warmth and sensuality into the small living area to the right. She noticed his iPod connected to a set of small speakers on one of the end tables, set to a slow and sexy song that was no doubt part of an entire playlist of songs just like it.

"In here, Lu."

She slid her feet from her sandals and padded farther into the room, looking for Reid. His voice, even lower than normal, came from the direction of the living room, but she didn't see him anywhere. Her stomach tightened into that knot, which was probably suffocating the things fluttering around in there. Screw butterflies. Those had to be hummingbirds. On speed.

Rounding the couch, she finally found Reid sitting on the floor in nothing but a pair of white athletic shorts, one leg stretched in front of him and the other bent with his forearm resting on his knee. He'd laid out the big floor pillows usually stacked in the corner and then complemented them with the decorative pillows from the couch and each of the beds. It looked like the floor of a sheikh with terrible taste in interior design, and yet, it was also the sexiest setup ever.

In one fluid motion he stood and held out his hand. Lucie swallowed hard and wiped her hands on her thighs in case they were grotesquely sweaty, and then placed her fingers in his. He pulled her into the center with him, but didn't pull her into his arms. There couldn't have been more than two inches between them, but it felt like the Grand Canyon.

She tilted her head up to meet his stare, and he angled his down to meet hers. It was then she realized he might be waiting for her to make the first move like in the workout room. *Okay, no problem. All you need to do is start things, Lucie.* She closed her eyes and tipped her face even more, waiting for the moment her lips would meet his, anticipation coursing through her veins like a drug...

But nothing happened.

Opening her eyes she wondered if time had somehow frozen. Reid hadn't moved a muscle— His jaw muscles jumped. God, that was sexy. Why was that so sexy? She wondered what it meant when he did that. Jackson always did it when he was aggravated. Was he aggravated?

"Reid?"

He said nothing at first, but lightly tapped the length of his finger over her lips once, as if to say he didn't want her to speak, then took it away again. She furrowed her brow. She didn't understand.

He walked around to her back, again so close but not touching. She felt his breaths on the side of her face as he leaned in. And when a single finger trailed down her arm, she swore an electric current burned in its wake. "Seduction isn't about actions," he said, retracing the path back toward her shoulder. "It's about control. I can make you do all the work—have you undress me, do a strip tease, even have you on your knees in front of me—and as long as I'm the one controlling the situation, you're actually the one being seduced."

Reid moved her hair over to fall in front on one side. God, she wanted him to pull her into his body, to feel his chest on the backs of her shoulders and the length of his erection cradled against her ass.

"Lose the shirt, Lucie."

Grabbing the hem in both hands, Lucie raised her arms, pulled it over her head, and tossed it onto the couch.

"Now the pants."

With shaking fingers she released the button, slid the zipper down, and let the capris fall to the floor before kicking them away. All that remained on her body was a white lace demibra and matching thong.

Finally Reid put more than a single finger on her and to feel the kiss he placed on the nape of her neck after teetering on the edge for all that time was like a jolt of lust shot straight through her. She jerked in response and there may have been a moan, she couldn't be sure. Her body, her brain, everything felt hyperaware and short-circuited all at the same time.

Her knees gave way, but strong hands grabbed her hips and pulled her back to hold her steady. "Shhhh. I've got you. I want you to lie on your stomach. Use the pillows however you want to make yourself comfortable."

He helped her down and once she was settled, joined her by stretching out alongside of her. With her face turned toward him she studied the intensity in his features as he ran his hand down her back, her waist, over the curve of one cheek. His jaw flexed, hollowing his cheeks with every tic, and his hazel eyes in the red-tinged light reminded her of the fiery colors of autumn.

"Damn, Lu. When did you get an ass like this?"

Was she supposed to answer him? He hadn't wanted her to talk earlier so she'd just assume it was a rhetorical question. Besides, she wouldn't even know *how* to answer that given the way her brain had shut down the minute he touched her.

All thoughts of questions and answers evaporated when a thick finger followed the line of her thong between her ass until it reached the sheer triangle covering her sex. Instinctively her hips raised off the floor, giving him better access. Apparently they had a mind all their own. Thankfully they were on the same page as her.

"Fuck you're so wet." Now two fingers

stroked back to front, and back again. Then he settled his upper body between her legs, which placed his face —

Lucie gasped as he bit her left cheek. Not hard enough to hurt, but enough to cause a quick sting of surprise before he kissed it better.

"I've never done that before," he said, "but there's something about your ass that makes me need to devour it. Did that bother you?"

"No," she said, lifting her hips off the pillow underneath, a silent beg for more.

"No," he agreed, kneading the opposite cheek with his callused palm. "I think you rather enjoyed it, didn't you?" The fingers of one hand returned to massage her swollen folds as the other continued to stroke and knead her ass and all she wanted was more.

Smack!

A strangled scream rent the air a split second after his hand left her butt. Again, her reaction was more from shock than pain.

"You didn't answer me, Lu." Answer him? She couldn't even remember her name at the moment, much less a question. Thankfully he repeated it. "Do you like what I'm doing to this pretty little ass of yours?"

"Yes," she exclaimed through another nip, this one closer to the crease near her thigh.

"Everything you're doing feels so good."

"It's a damn good thing because I'm really digging seeing my marks on your skin, sweetheart."

Before she had a chance to respond, Reid grabbed the thin strap that banded her waist in both hands and yanked in opposite directions, rending the silk in two.

"I'll buy you more."

She didn't know why, but the idea of Reid needing to replace a pair of her underwear every time he ripped it from her body struck her as funny. She giggled. Until his tongue laved her sex in a warm, wet stripe.

"*Ohmigod.*"

Now it was his turn to be amused and the vibrations from his lips tingled her nerve-rich skin and coaxed more juices as she clenched inside. "Turn over so I can do this properly."

She rolled to her back and stared up as he held himself above her. "I don't know that the word 'proper' works in this context. I think the adverb you're looking for is 'illicitly.'"

"You're right. Illicit definitely describes my plans for you. But you're also wrong."

"About what?"

"There's still a proper way to perform illicit acts." With a wicked grin and a devilish glint in his eye he said, "And I'm going to show you exactly what I mean."

• • •

Reid soaked up her innocent reaction like the desert would a long-awaited rain. He'd never been with anyone like her. He'd always dated fast and ready girls who knew what they were doing and what he was about: no-strings-attached sex.

Lucie was refreshing and so damn responsive. He loved keeping her on the edge, always wondering what he'd do next, and then shocking her—and sometimes even himself—with his next move.

He lowered himself so he was partially draped over her, but still held himself up enough that he wasn't crushing her with his weight. She was such a little slip of a thing, fine and delicate and utterly beautiful. He couldn't understand why she thought herself so plain.

Her soft gray eyes encompassed by a charcoal-colored ring gazed at him with the unfocused sight lust was known to induce. He brushed the fringe of her bangs to the side and noticed the tiny heart-shaped freckle. He bent his head and kissed it and her eyes fluttered shut on a sigh as he then kissed a path to her mouth.

Using pressure he encouraged her to open

and swept his tongue through to find hers. The feel of her tongue sliding with his, moving over and around as their lips laid claim to the other was the headiest feeling. Her hands came up to frame his ribs and when he rocked his hips, grinding his cock against her, her fingers dug into his sides. The sharp bite of her nails scratching his skin turned him on something fierce.

The lace of her bra rasped against his sensitive nipples and he groaned as they tightened from the sensation. As good as it felt, he'd rather have it gone. Reaching behind her with one hand he expertly unhooked the clasp, pulled it off from the front, and whipped it somewhere behind him as he got his first glimpse of her bare breasts.

"Phenomenal," he rasped. And they were.

They were the perfect size for his hand; small enough to be perky and big enough to have that curved swell on the bottom from their weight. The first thing he thought of was the need to sculpt them. He'd spend hours getting everything just right. Her small, dusky rose nipples that puckered when he circled them with the tip of his finger. The gentle slope from her delicate clavicle to the tip of her nipple. The fullness underneath that grew even more under the heat of his stare.

Not wasting another second he bent to place moist kisses around the base of a breast. She arched her back and her breathing quickened. With his tongue he drew lazy patterns, but was careful to stay away from the center, driving her closer to that edge once more. After a minute or so he inched his way closer, now tracing the outer line of her areola.

Lucie made a frustrated noise and grabbed his head, trying to direct him to her nipple, but again Reid made her wait. Though she'd never believe him, holding back from taking her breast was almost just as torturous for him. At last he opened wide and drew as much of her as he could into his mouth. He lashed at her nipple with his tongue and sucked on her like she was his favorite hard candy. She cried out and arched into him until her back was bowed. Finally he pulled his head back until she was released from his lips with a wet pop. Her tight, reddened bud gave him the same high as knowing he'd won a round in one of his fights and gave him the same motivation to do it again.

He repeated the entire process on the other side, worshiping her breast with his mouth while his hands roamed over her satin skin. When he was certain he'd won round two as well, he released her breast and homed in on the location of his next conquest.

Raising up on his knees, he used his hands to push her legs further apart. Her dark pink lips glistened with her honey. Unable to resist, he parted them with his thumbs to gaze at the source. He'd never studied a woman like this before and was surprised he could actually see her inner walls tightening, desperate for something to hold on to.

Dragging his gaze away he saw the self-conscious look in her eyes. "You're absolutely gorgeous. But you look too empty." Holding her gaze he slid his thumbs in to circle the rim of her opening. "Want something to fill you up?"

She no sooner gave him a nod than he plunged both of his thumbs inside as far as they could go. She cried out as her pelvis shot off the pillows, her hands fisting in the ones unlucky enough to be under them. Her response fueled the fire inside of him until his core felt molten. When her hips lowered once more he rewarded her by thrusting his thumbs, putting pressure on her inner walls with every withdrawal.

He watched as her juices ran out, dripping down the crevice to her ass, and a deep thirst for her suddenly overwhelmed him. Repositioning himself lower, Reid began kissing her inner thighs.

"No, you don't have to—"

"Yes, I do." If he didn't get his mouth on her in the next few seconds, he'd go crazy. "I really do."

Just as he was about to descend, her hand

cupped his chin preventing him from going anywhere. "No, what I mean is, it doesn't do anything for me, so you don't have to do it."

It took him several seconds to process what she'd just said. It doesn't *do anything* for her? Either her ex was a total fuckup in the oral department or—no, he wasn't even going to finish that. He'd bet his UFC contract the dude was a fuckup.

He encircled her wrist, pulled her hand from his face, and placed a kiss in her palm as he stared into her eyes. He needed her to see the truth in his as he spoke. "I need to taste you, Lucie. I'm dying to have you on my tongue, in my mouth. And I will guarantee that what I'm about to do will do plenty for you."

Reid didn't give her the chance to debate the outcome with him. He dipped down and licked a path from the bottom all the way up, adding a bit of pressure when he got to her clit. She cried out and her hips tried to jackknife, but he held her in place so she couldn't screw with his aim. She tasted like the sweetest of nectars. He could happily spend the rest of the night between her legs.

Over, around, and straight up the middle, he kept his tongue in constant motion, breaking it up with kisses and nibbles. He paid attention to every moan, every whimper, learning what she liked and what drove her positively fricking insane.

Sweat covered her body, her breasts heaved with her short breaths, her head thrown back and eyes squeezed tight. She was a sight like no other, writhing in the throes of passion. But there was something that would make it even better. For both of them.

"Lucie, baby." He waited for the rasp of his voice to penetrate her lust-clouded mind. A moment later her lashes fluttered and her silver irises stared back at him. "Raise yourself up on your elbows. I want you to watch what I'm doing to this sweet pussy of yours."

Slowly she did as he asked until she was propped up. With her legs bent and spread wide and her ass on a large pillow she had the perfect view. She'd been close to the edge before he'd stopped. Now it was time to bring her right to it and keep her there until she begged him to bring her over the other side. A devilish smile lifted a corner of his mouth as he once again sank between her legs.

This time he made sure to keep his head angled to the side so he didn't block her view. With the tip of his tongue he teased her outer lips for several strokes before finally burrowing in to find the swollen nub that had her raking in a sharp breath at first contact.

Adding to the sensation he slid a thick finger deep into her pussy and pumped it in and out as his tongue alternately circled around and flicked over her clit. Her eyes looked like liquid silver on fire. Her breathing became labored through parted lips.

"Oh, God...*Reid*." She started shaking her head. "I can't— You have to—"

Almost there. So close. He added another finger and pursed his lips over her clit, applying pulses of suction.

"Ah!" Her hips moved, grinding her pussy against his face, and he knew she was at the point where she couldn't control them even if she wanted to. She was firmly balanced at the edge of climax, just where he wanted her.

"Come for me, Lucie," he ordered. "Let me drink your honey."

He increased the pace of his thrusts with his fingers, reveling in the juices that coated them. Locking his lips over the bundle of nerves again, he worked it with his tongue. Seconds later, at just the right moment, he lightly clamped his teeth on it, finally pulling her over into the abyss where her body shattered and she screamed his name to the heavens.

The walls of her sheath squeezed his fingers as she came down from her climax, simultaneously lowering herself to lay spent on the pillows. Too bad he wasn't nearly done with her. His cock was hard as a sledgehammer and he had every intention of finding his release in her body. With a quick reach over to the side, he retrieved the condom he'd set out and had himself covered before she even knew he'd moved.

"Lucie?"

She kept her eyes closed and had a sated look on her face. He smiled when he thought about how short-lived her satiation would be once he worked her up again.

"Hmm?"

"I was just wondering if that did anything for you."

Her eyes flew open. "Not really, no. What else have you got, hotshot?"

He narrowed his eyes at her as he hooked an arm under one of her knees and lifted to open her wide to him. "You realize you're on very dangerous ground, don't you? Not only did you insult my sexual prowess, you also challenged a highly competitive athlete."

She gave him a heart-stopping smile and said, "Then I guess you'd better prove yourself."

"Oh, I'll prove myself all right. Consider yourself warned, sweetheart. You asked for it."

Continuing to hold her one leg up and to the

side, Reid lined up his throbbing cock with her tight, dripping pussy and sat himself balls, deep in one hard thrust of his hips. A mix between a grunt and a moan rent the air from her.

"Holy shit, you're so big."

He wasn't a conceited ass when it came to his dick, but it wasn't the first time he'd heard a woman say that. However, coming from Lucie, he suddenly felt like He-Man, minus the fur underwear. He also felt as big as she claimed. He'd never been inside a woman so tight, so perfect a fit for him. Unable to hold still any longer he withdrew almost completely, pushed all the way back in, and then set a slow and steady rhythm to bring them to their peaks gradually.

She instinctively rolled her hips up to meet each of his thrusts, adding to the waves of sensation emanating from his cock to swirl around in his balls and settle at the base of his spine.

"Goddamn you feel good, woman." Looking down at where their bodies joined, Reid got an eyeful of the hottest thing he'd ever seen. Her slick lips sucked at his cock each time he pulled away and coated them with her sweet cream every time he rocked forward.

He hadn't been aware she was watching the same thing until he heard her say, "That's so hot."

"Hell yeah, it is." Even more so now that he

knew she liked the look of him driving into her. Needing to take as much of her as he could, he released her leg in favor of bracing himself over her on his forearms. He picked up speed as he captured her mouth with his, fucking her mouth with his tongue in tandem with his lower half.

Their sweat-soaked bodies slid over one another, the sounds of flesh meeting flesh in several places and heavy breathing peppered with moans filled the air. Lucie wrenched her mouth from his, lifting her chin and inciting him to move to her neck to continue his goal of devouring her whole.

"I'm so close. I can't believe I'm going to—*uhn*—again."

He smiled against her throat when her grunt took the place of the word "come" when he'd added a twist of his hips to a thrust. Taking his cue from that, he did it again. And again. And again. Until she was calling out his name over and over between pleas to stop and never-ever stop.

Sneaking one hand between their bodies, he easily found her swollen clit with the pad of his thumb and dragged it over the top of it with one last hard thrust. He wasn't typically vocal during sex, but he couldn't have held back his groan if his life had been threatened when they came together, her pussy convulsing around him as he spent himself in powerful spurts.

As they came back to each other over the next several minutes of harsh breathing and muscles collapsing, Reid recognized that sex with Lucie blew all of his other experiences out of the water. It didn't matter that he'd had wilder sex, longer sex, or kinkier sex than what they'd just had. There was a huge difference. Miles and miles of difference. He just couldn't pinpoint the why of it, and he was too exhausted to try.

Carefully, Reid pulled out of her and wrapped the condom in the paper towel he'd placed off to the side to dispose of it in the morning. Then he settled himself on the bed of pillows, pulled a blanket over them, and wrapped her in his arms. Her head fell naturally into the dip between his chest and shoulder and her arm banded around his stomach. Within seconds he heard the soft sound of snoring and felt her body lose all tension as she drifted off to sleep. And with a grin on his face from a happiness he didn't fully understand, he wasn't far behind.

CHAPTER TWELVE

Lucie sat on her couch, curled up with her book, and once again stared at the pages without seeing a single word. But this time, instead of her stomach in knots from anxiety, she caught herself smiling like a total idiot from what she could only describe as giddiness. Her night with Reid had been so impassioned, so all-consuming, that she'd been on the longest sexual high of her life all day.

When she'd woken up that morning he'd already started his stretching exercises. She'd been terrified things would be awkward between them, that in the garish light of day he'd have realized his mistake and wished he could take it all back. Her plan had been to avoid him until she had time to think, to batten down the hatches on her stupid girlie emotions that made her unable to regret even the one night with him.

Wrapping the soft throw blanket around her and tucking it under her arms, Lucie held her breath and did her best Invisible Man impression as she passed the workout room.

"About time you woke up, sleepyhead." Lucie froze in midtiptoe as his strong arms banded around her from behind. She knew he was shirtless by the way his chest warmed her upper back not covered by the blanket. "Why did it look like you were trying to sneak by me?" he asked before nudging her hair aside with his chin so he could place moist kisses along her neck.

"I…um…" *What did he ask? Crap.*

Suddenly his body tensed. "Do you regret last night, Luce?"

Before she spoke Lucie prayed her damn nerves stayed out of her voice. "Do you?"

He turned her around and tipped her chin up. His eyes looked more on the light brown side in the morning light. "I'm not going to lie. The sex was amazing, and I *never* regret amazing sex with an amazing woman." He gave a small sigh as he studied her face and tucked her hair behind her ear. "But I don't want to compromise our friendship either."

"No, of course." She cleared her throat and tried to keep her eyes from shifting away as they rejected the coming lies. "I mean, it's definitely best we keep it to a one-time thing."

"Right." His eyes fell to her lips. He licked his own with the flick of his tongue. "We don't want to make things weird between us. After all, you're on your way to dating your doctor and soon I'll be back in Vegas."

The shine on his lips transfixed her gaze and the rhythm of her pulse kept time with the seconds that passed before she remembered it was her turn to refute the idea of a phenomenal no-strings attached sexcapade with one of the hottest men in sports, not to mention her childhood crush. But she couldn't think of a single thing to say.

"Luce," he rasped, his hands settling on her hips, his eyes never leaving her mouth. "We shouldn't…right?"

She tried to respond, her mouth opening several times to say something, anything. Finally she gave up and settled for grabbing the back of his head in one hand and kissing him senseless.

Reid responded in kind, yanking her into his body and taking control of the kiss with a simple angle adjustment and thrust of his tongue. It was a well-coordinated attack she had no defense for, even if she wanted one.

He pushed her back against the wall, grinding his body into hers, which skewed the blanket into a bunched-up mess between them. Reid, being the gentleman he was, helped her with her creative wardrobe mishap by shoving it to the floor. Problem solved.

Breaking the kiss he moved his mouth over her jawline, following it back to that sensitive spot behind her ear. One hand cupped a breast; the other squeezed her ass like he was holding on for dear life. His thick erection rubbed against her clit through the mesh of his shorts creating delicious friction and making her lose her mind.

"Oh, God, Reid," she panted. "What are we doing? This is crazy."

"No," he argued, biting her earlobe and making her gasp from the strange pleasure-pain she was only beginning to learn about. "*This* is foreplay." He sucked her earlobe into his mouth for a brief, hot moment, and then said, "The fact that I can't keep my goddamn hands off you is crazy."

"That, too." Just as they were about to lose their minds in each other, her cell phone started playing "Jackson" by Johnny Cash. "Shit! It's my brother."

Reid pulled back and gave her a you've-gotta-be-kidding-me look, but Lucie snatched the blanket off the floor and tucked it around her as she raced for her phone. Her brother was worse than a mother hen and if she didn't answer, he'd be calling her grandmotherly neighbor to come and check on her.

Flipping the phone open she said, "Hey, Jackson. What's up?"

"Since when does something have to be 'up' for me to call my little sister? And why do you sound like you just raced to the phone?"

"Uh, because I did. I'd forgotten it in my room so I ran to get to it because I know how you are. I didn't want you to have to call the cavalry for no reason."

"I'd hardly call Mrs. Egan a cavalry," he answered wryly. "Besides, the last time I asked her to check on you she brought you fresh brownies. I can see how that'd be a huge burden to bear for your brother's peace of mind."

"Fine, I suppose you have a poin—*ah*!" Reid's large hand had startled the crap out of her when it reached under the blanket to her stomach, and now it was snaking its way toward her breasts.

"What's wrong?"

She slapped Reid's hand and pushed it away. When he chuckled in amusement she glared at him in warning, but it didn't seem to faze him in the least. "Nothing, Jax, I just, um…" *Think, girl, think.* "…stubbed my toe on the coffee table."

Jackson's smile came through the telephone.

"Still as klutzy as ever, huh? Good to know some things don't change."

Her hair was moved to the side before a hot mouth seared her neck with moist kisses and the occasional scrape of teeth. A throbbing deep in her core sent shockwaves of tingling through her body with every beat. Her limbs weakened. Her arm didn't want to hold the phone up to her ear, and her legs didn't want to hold her up at all. And what the hell had she been saying? *Klutzy! That's it.* "Yeah, well, it would be nice if that…you know…ah, thing…could change, er…whatever."

"Hey, are you feeling all right?" Jackson asked. "You sound strange."

Reid licked the shell of her ear and whispered, "Get him off the phone, or I'll get *you* off with him on it."

The idea of messing around while listening to her brother was like standing under a bucket of ice water balanced on a ledge with a string that said Pull Here. Nooooo thank you.

"Actually, Jackson, can I call you back later? I really did a number on my toe and I need to go put ice on it and stuff." She did the requisite pauses and "uh-huhs" as he wrapped up his brotherly advice on how to care for a sprained toe and how to know if it was broken, yadda yadda. Finally, he finished, and she was pulling the phone away from her ear before she even gave him a rushed, "Okayloveyoutoo."

Just as she finished her incoherent babbling and dropped the phone to the couch, Reid's hand slid down to her sex. Without pause he plunged two of his fingers deep inside her while his free hand reclaimed one of her breasts. A myriad of sensations crashed over her all at once. His rough palm abraded her taut nipple and his fingers ignited toe-curling pleasure deep within her as they thrust over and over into her body.

Her head pressed into his chest as she arched her back and brought her hands behind her head to sink her nails into his shoulders. He hissed in a breath at her ear. She knew he loved the sting from her nails and teeth and she was no longer shy about giving it to him. He reciprocated with a pinch and pull of her nipple, the sensation like fireworks in her chest.

"Ah, yes!"

"That's it, baby. God, you feel so hot. Come for me. I want to feel your body sucking my fingers deep inside you."

His words were the accelerant on the flames of passion burning within her, causing an instant wildfire. With one final thrust of his hand and the feeling of his teeth sinking into the taut cord in her neck, Lucie flew apart, shattering completely until she was sure she no longer stood on the normal plane of existence with the rest of the world.

When she finally managed to turn around, she eagerly stroked him over his shorts, but he quickly grabbed her wrist and pulled her hand away. "Hold on."

"What's wrong?"

"As much as I would *love* to finish this, if I take you to bed—or to couch, floor, kitchen table, or anything else—I'll keep us there all day and we'll get nothing accomplished."

Lucie felt herself nod even though her body was giving the order to pounce. "You're right, we have…uh, things, like…"

The corner of his mouth hitched up. "Exercises, training, boring stuff like that."

"Right, yes, thank you."

"You're welcome. Why don't you go do whatever you do in the mornings, and you can meet me in the workout room when you're done."

She wasn't entirely sure she was retaining everything he said. She still felt like she was coming down from an incredible high, but she figured it was probably safe to agree with whatever he suggested. "Excellent idea. I'll just go do…that."

He chuckled low in his chest—his wonderfully

bare, ridged with muscles chest—and turned her toward her bedroom. Then with a light slap on her ass, he ordered her to get a move on.

Somehow they managed to keep from groping each other while they finished his PT exercises and their regular workouts. Then they spent the rest of the day figuring out how to alter Reid's normal strenuous training exercises to accommodate his healing injury so he could stay in fighting shape.

After taking her shower, she sat on the couch waiting for him to finish his so they could relax together and watch a movie after a long day. She'd intended on reading, but the only thing in her mind at the moment was a splendidly naked Reid Andrews with water sluicing over his body. As her body heat shot through the roof, she turned her book sideways and turned it into a fan. *At least I'm using it for something.*

When she heard the bathroom door open, she quickly put the book back in front of her face and pretended to look for all the world that she hadn't just been on the path to imagining doing wicked things to him under the hot spray of water. Nope, nothing lewd going on in her brain. She was simply doing some light reading. Totally. Innocent.

"Whoa. That book must have some pretty hot scenes in it."

Her eyes flew up to his as he took his seat next to her on the couch. "What makes you say that?"

"Because your cheeks are flushed and you have a crease in your lower lip from biting it." He cupped her chin in his hand and used the pad of his thumb to drag it across her swollen lip. "Which I now know is something you do when you're incredibly turned on. Are you turned on, Lucie?"

So much for totally innocent.

• • •

"I've been wanting to see *Warrior*."

Reid dropped his hand and smiled at her abrupt change in topic. He couldn't help it. One night of curl-your-toes sex and an orgasm in her living room later and she was still shy with him.

She put her book on the end table and fidgeted with a couch pillow. "It's about two brothers who enter the same MMA competition and have to fight each other."

"I know. I've seen it."

"Oh," she said, frowning.

"But I'd like to see it again. I watched it with several of the guys from the gym and they were pretty obnoxious, so I missed a lot of it." That wasn't actually true, but a small lie to smooth the crease in her brow was worth it. Her smile was a bonus.

"Great. Okay, you cue it up and I'll make the popcorn."

She practically bounced off the couch with excitement. One second she was crossing in front of him on her way to the kitchen, and the next he heard a *thump* and *oof* as she crumpled to the ground at his feet.

"Whoa there, Lubert." He picked her up and sat her next to him with her legs over his lap. "You didn't notice that coffee table, or what?"

She glared at him as she sucked in air through a clenched jaw and fisted her hands in front of her. "Oh, man, why does stubbing your toes hurt so bad? Owie, owie, owie."

"Here, let me hold it for you." He carefully placed the toes of her right foot between his palms and pressed to keep a light pressure on them. When he realized they'd been sitting like that for quite some time, he raised his head to find her studying his hands, eyes shimmering with unshed tears. "Hey," he said softly, cupping her cheek. "Does it hurt that badly? Maybe you broke something."

Lucie gave an almost imperceptible shake of her head. "That's what my mom always said when we banged ourselves up. 'Hold it.' I always thought it was a silly thing to say, but it always helped."

"Are you kidding? It was a brilliant thing to say. You know how many times I've 'held it' after getting knocked around in grappling exercises? Hundreds, if not thousands. And it always helps." With a half grin he added, "Either that or an ice bath. It's a toss-up, really. Comes down to how much time I have."

She snorted at the ridiculous statement and followed it with a nervous laugh and her hand clapped over her face. Reid pulled her hand down. "I like it when you snort."

"Oh, shut up," she said with a playful shove before swinging her feet to the floor. "I don't mean to do it, you know."

"I know, that's why it's so damn adorable."

Stopping at the edge of the couch she turned and narrowed those gray pixie eyes at him. "*No one* thinks a girl snorting is adorable."

He shrugged and lifted his arms to lay on the back of the couch. "I would've agreed with that statement until I heard you do it over a week ago."

She shook her head and laughed on her way to the kitchen, clearly not believing him, but that was okay. She would one day. One day soon she was going to know her worth and be comfortable with everything about herself, including her tendency to snort and run into inanimate objects.

As she made the popcorn and got them drinks, he went through the movies offered on cable, selected *Warrior*, and paused it as soon as it came on. "Hey," he called out. "You know what you call stubbing your toe just now?"

"The same thing I call it every time I do something like that: clumsiness."

"No, this time it's called karma. For when you lied to your brother this morning about stubbing your toe."

She poked her head around the doorway, eyes wide. "Oh my gosh, you're right! Well, that sucks." Disappearing back into the kitchen she said, "Remind me to never make up lies that involve personal bodily harm in the future."

He was still laughing when she walked back into the room holding a big bowl of popcorn and two bottles of water. "You just need to adjust your lies accordingly so that when karma does come around, as the saying goes, it's something you'll enjoy."

She managed to place the bowl on the low table in front of them and sit on the couch without any further mishaps. As she settled back into the cushions she asked, "Oh, yeah? Like what?"

Twisting his body to face her, Reid leaned in close. "Like, 'I'm sorry, I can't talk right now because Reid's licking my breasts like they're his own personal ice cream cones.'" He'd never seen someone's cheeks pinken so fast. Getting a rise out of her was quickly becoming one of his favorite past times and he couldn't help taking it even further. "Although, I'm not sure if that falls under karma so much as it does contributing to the universe's suggestion box." He lowered his eyes to the juncture of her thighs hidden by the small black pajama shorts. "Speaking of boxes—"

That was all the further he got before she'd silenced him with a hand over his mouth. Though she was doing her best at looking incredulous, she was having a damn hard time hiding her smile. "Reid Michael Andrews! What's gotten into you?"

He pulled her hand away as he laughed. "It must be you because I haven't had this much fun with a girl in forever."

She tipped her head in a coy manner and looked up at him through those sexy spiked lashes. "Then again, technically speaking, I suppose it's *you* that's gotten into *me*." Reid hadn't been aware his jaw had dropped until she lifted it up with the tips of her fingers and said, "You keep your mouth open like that and you're bound to catch flies." Then with a cat-who-ate-the-canary grin she pulled the popcorn bowl into her lap.

Reid burst out in a long, hard laugh as he slung an arm around her and tucked her into his side. He started the movie and they fell into a comfortable silence, eating popcorn and relaxing with each other. His attention seemed more focused on her rather than the drama on the screen, though. He noticed during the fighting scenes that her whole body tensed up. If something surprised her, she'd utter a quiet gasp. And while watching an on-screen kiss, her fingertips drifted up to lightly touch her own lips as though she could feel it as much as the characters.

Lucie was a quiet woman by nature. She'd lived her life standing in the wings, content to let those around her take center stage. But that didn't mean she was any less passionate than those who preferred the spotlight. She loved her job and her friends, was fiercely dedicated and loyal, and a romantic at heart.

Reid knew he'd never settle down and have a family. He didn't have the "family man gene" like most people. Beyond that, he didn't live the sort of life that families flourished in.

His dad was Stan Andrews, one of the top

professional boxers in his day. He'd fought many of the greats and even won against some of them. His mother had been one of the ring bunnies that hung around the gym, went to all the fights, and did her best to land a fighter. Reid's parents had been happy until he was five. That's when the great Stan Andrews got hit one too many times in the head, and it ended his career. After that he started drinking, and his wife was disgusted with having a washed-up ex-boxer as a husband. The thrill of being ringside and cheering in his corner was gone. And then so was she.

She'd left her son with a man who had no idea how to raise a child. In fact, he hadn't known how to do anything other than drink and fight. So instead of raising a son, he trained a fighter.

Reid couldn't resent the training his father had given him. He'd been tough, sometimes to the point of extremes, but in the end it had been all worth it. He became one of the best light-heavyweight mixed martial arts fighters in the world and got fame and fortune out of the deal. He lived a damn good life back in Vegas, doing one of the things he loved.

But the part of him that wasn't a fighter—the part that wanted to sculpt, that wanted to be a son—that was the part that resented his father and everything he stood for. Only it hadn't done any good for that part of him to rebel. He'd learned as a kid that begging for anything more than a fighter/trainer relationship with his father was hopeless. And as a teenager he'd learned that pursuing any hobbies that took time away from his training schedule was pointless.

So, no, Reid didn't even have a chance at being relationship material, much less family material. He only looked into the future as far as his next fight. Until someone's hand was raised in the cage, he ate, slept, and breathed everything he needed to prepare for going up against his opponent. And afterward, he started all over again for the next fight. Always a fighter. Never a spectator.

When Lucie jerked with a gasp at seeing a particularly bloody punch, he set the popcorn bowl aside and adjusted until he sat sideways on the couch and she curled up on her side between his legs with her head on his chest. He tried damn hard not to notice how much he liked the way she snuggled into him, rubbing her cheek on his T-shirt to get just the right spot she wanted.

Smiling, he played with her hair, picking up sections and running his fingers through the length, loving the silky feeling and the flowery scent that he now associated with only her.

He wasn't sure how much time had passed,

but before the movie ended Lucie's breathing had become deep and even with sleep. Grabbing the throw blanket from the back of the couch he tucked it around her and settled into the corner more to get comfortable.

"Sweet dreams, Lu." He kissed the top of her hair and didn't even remember closing his eyes.

CHAPTER THIRTEEN

Reid sank into the overstuffed couch cushions, turning sideways to stretch out his legs and lean back against the pillows he'd shoved against the side. He'd just finished showering after a long fucking day and all he wanted to do was lie there and drink the one ice-cold beer he was allowing himself for the night.

Another week had gone by since his relaxing movie night with Lucie, but instead of the fun and games they'd had time for the previous week, the last seven days had been more stressful than anything. When they weren't working on his shoulder and training, he'd been at publicity junkets, and Lucie was getting called into work to help out with special-needs cases.

The only bright spots were the quickies they somehow found time for. But where they lacked in duration, the sessions more than made up for in passion. Any time he and Lucie got hot and heavy, it was like a chemical reaction ending with an inevitable explosion that rocked them to their cores.

During one such occasion they realized they were out of condoms, prompting a frank—albeit hurried—discussion about protection. Since they both had clean bills of health and Lucie had gotten a form of birth control implanted in her arm at her ex's request that lasted several years, they decided to forgo the latex for the duration of their time together.

The memory of sinking into her that first time with nothing between them made his balls ache. Her slick heat had set him ablaze, igniting every cell in his body as her channel milked his bare cock until he'd spilled himself deep inside her. It had taken them longer than usual to come down from that lovemaking, but when they did, his elation had shone in her eyes too.

Unfortunately, their daytime interludes were the only ones they'd had all week. By the time either of them got home at night they had just enough energy to shower and fall into bed.

Reid had a suspicion that Mann had asked her to come in just so he could see Lucie. Maybe he wanted to see if her transformation extended beyond the one night at the restaurant. Maybe he just wanted an excuse to see her and flash his girlie dimples at her, who the fuck knew.

What he *did* know, was that he'd been unable to do anything about it. Once the UFC found out from Butch that Reid was up in Reno getting special training and therapy for his injury, they'd set up press conferences and publicity signings, and he'd had no option but to do them. It was part of his contract.

It'd been damn hard to focus, though, knowing that while he was answering the same questions he'd answered dozens of times, Lucie was being ogled by that surgeon. Maybe even groped if he'd had the chance. Shit, he hadn't thought of that before. Had Mann kissed her already? Then again, it didn't really matter. She was getting ready to leave on a date with the guy even as he lay there, so she was as good as kissed by the end of the night.

Reid's hand tightened on the beer bottle and his jaw clenched.

A bang and clatter came from the bathroom down the hallway. "Shit!"

He turned his head in the direction of the commotion. "Everything okay in there?"

"Yeah," she said dejectedly. "I just knocked my knee on the vanity and put a run in my pantyhose, and it's my only pair."

"You want me to run you to the drugstore down the street?" Then maybe he'd accidentally take a wrong turn on the way back making her late and Mann would think she stood him up and lose interest due to his fragile ego.

"No, that's okay, there's no time. I'll just go without."

Go without? The guy would have access to her bare legs. All it would take is a brush of his hand under the table linen and he'd be able to do all sorts of creative things even though they were in public. He'd know; he'd done it plenty of times when he got bored during required dinners with the upper echelon of the fighting world.

"Why don't you just wear a pantsuit?"

He heard the clacking of heels on the wooden floor and then she rounded the corner where he could see her. Immediately his mouth began to salivate like the ripest strawberry he'd ever seen dangled right in front of his face. That's what she reminded him of.

Bright red from boobs to butt, she was striking in a simple cocktail dress. Spaghetti straps so small as to practically be nonexistent, a neckline that dipped into the space between her breasts, and a hem that flirted around her thighs, mere inches from the curves of her butt.

She'd curled her hair into large ringlets that gave her a smoking just-been-tumbled look and her makeup was noticeable, but subtle, with the exception of the matching red lipstick.

Affection between them right before she went on a date with another guy seemed all kinds of wrong, and he'd figured it was better to avoid it than analyze it, so he'd planned on keeping things platonic for the evening.

But the image of those juicy lips wrapped around a certain part of his anatomy bombed an RPG-sized hole right through the Appropriate Dam he'd constructed in his brain.

"I don't own a pantsuit, Reid. You never picked one out for me to try on."

Of course he didn't. What guy wanted to see a girl in an ugly-ass pantsuit? His eye had been drawn to every single tiny dress he could find. What a fucking moron he was.

"Doesn't this look okay? Is it too much?" she asked while trying to get a good look at herself by twisting her body in all sorts of directions. Just then her intercom buzzed, sounding like an air horn in the otherwise quiet apartment. "Oh, God, I'm so nervous. I can't do this. I'm going to tell him I can't go. Claim I have food poisoning or a spontaneous case of pancreatitis."

He was so close to agreeing with her. So

goddamn close. But in the end, he couldn't do it. Just because he was experiencing some strange and juvenile bout of jealousy over her didn't mean he had the right to sabotage her impending happiness with Dr. Perfect Dimples.

Kicking his inner caveman back into his cave, he stood and crossed to her. "Here," he said, handing her the bottle. "Drink some of this and relax. You're not canceling the date and wasting all this effort I've put into being your fairy godmother."

She placed a hand over her stomach as though trying to quiet the butterflies inside while the other accepted the beer and polished it off in less than five seconds. So much for his one beer.

Handing him the empty, she said, "Thanks, I needed to hear that."

"Because you like picturing me with wings and a magic wand?" he said with a smirk.

She laughed, looking more at ease every second. "No, you dumb jock, because I needed the encouragement to actually go through with this."

Encouragement? Reid sobered and studied her face, trying to see if there was something—anything—he might be missing. The buzzer rang again and even though it sounded identical to the first time, he swore the man's impatience from two floors below somehow changed the pitch.

Aggravated at the interruption he took the two strides to the door, depressed the intercom button and barked, "We hear you, hold on," before returning to her.

When he spoke, it was quiet, deliberate. "You don't need encouragement, Lu, because this is what you've wanted all along. What you've done all of this for…right?"

She stared back at him, her eyes tracking back and forth between his, her lips slightly parted as if ready to respond as soon as her brain could wrap itself around an answer. The low levels of tension from her nerves and his *whatever* it was slowly began to climb until it was a palpable essence choking the space between them.

With his empty hand he reached up and lifted a curl that had fallen over her eye and set it back with the others where it belonged. Her gaze fell to his lips; it was a cue he didn't miss. Reid was seriously starting to think the role of gentleman was way overrated. But if he was going to make a move, he had to be sure.

"Lucie? Do you want to go on this date with him?"

"I—"

She was cut off by the theme song to *Rocky* coming from the kitchen. It took him a second to realize it was his cell phone. Lucie had insisted on giving all of his speed dial contacts personal ringers and they'd had a blast laughing and joking around as they searched for the perfect song for each of them. She'd picked that one for Butch.

Reid felt the muscle in his jaw work. *Nice timing, old man.* Was the whole universe in on some sort of conspiracy against them?

Then it him like a full right hook to the temple: yeah, it was. The universe was trying to remind him that he had no right to string her along with some fantasy of something that would never come true. He was acting like a selfish prick. Wanting to keep Lucie all to himself for the time he had her.

Until the time when he'd walk away from her.

He needed his ass kicked. "You'd better go," he said as he stepped out of her personal space. Walking toward the kitchen and his phone he called back over his shoulder to her. "Have fun on your date, Lubert. Don't forget to flirt with the waiter."

As he hit the button to call Butch back he heard the door open and close again and he suddenly felt sick to his stomach.

"Shoulda known better than to drink a beer while cutting weight." He put the phone to his ear and scoffed. He'd thought by saying it out loud it would sound more convincing than it did in his head. "That's what you get for thinking, dumbass."

"Andrews?" Butch's gravelly voice coming through the cell eased him to a degree. The man was more of a father to him than his real one ever had been. Ironic, considering his trainer and father could essentially switch roles in his life and it would be more accurate than what they were intended to be.

"Hey, Butch. Sorry I didn't get to the phone right away. What's up? How're the guys?"

"The boys are the same as ever. But I didn't call to chat about the boys. I have some good news."

He grabbed a water bottle from the fridge and walked back into the living room to resume his prone position on the couch. "Good, because I could really use some good news right about now."

"Scotty's coming back. Things progressed back home quicker than anticipated and he's due to arrive in Vegas in a week."

Reid shot back off the couch. He hadn't had a clue what Butch's good news was going to be, but being able to go home a month sooner than anticipated hadn't even crossed his mind.

"So you can get outta there and come on home. Train with your teammates and prepare for your championship fight in your own gym. Christ, if I know you, you're probably going nuts cooped up out there."

Butch wasn't entirely wrong. He had been getting restless lately. *Really* restless. But he didn't think it had to do with not being in his own surroundings and having the freedom to do as he pleased as much as it was not having any quality time with Lucie. In the short time they'd been thrown together, he'd come to look forward to just being with her. Whether it was sitting quietly at the table in the morning as he drank his protein shake and she sipped her coffee, or arguing over who got the remote based on who owned it versus who was the elder.

"Son, did you hear what I said?"

Reid cleared his throat and dragged a hand over his face. "Yeah, Butch, I heard you. That's great that Scotty's going to be back. I'm sure some of the other guys could use him, too."

"Well, yeah, but he'll still have most of his time blocked off to work with you. He knows what this fight means to your career."

"And I appreciate that, but you know, Luce has taken her vacation time to help me—"

"Luce? Who's that? What happened to that Miller lady?"

"That's who I'm talking about. Her name is Lucie. I'm just saying that I think it would be unprofessional if I took her dedication for granted and bailed sooner than planned."

Radio silence. *Shit*. Butch was a mild-mannered guy...until you said or did something against him that had to do with training, and the silence was the calm before the storm. It was his only similarity to Reid's father, but even then Butch never took it to the point of cruelty Stan Andrews had.

"Are you fucking kidding me! Am I being Plunk'd or whatever the hell it's called? Because I'm having a hard time understanding why my star fighter is turning down help from his *professional* trainer and *professional* sports doc to prepare for *the* biggest fight in his career!"

Reid started pacing in the small room like a caged lion in front of the dude with the whip. "Damn it, Butch, don't start on me like that, all right? I just said—"

"I heard what you said. What I'm concerned with, boy, is what you're *not* saying."

"What the hell is that supposed to mean?"

"It means the Reid I know would jump all over the chance to come back to camp and focus on taking back his belt. It means I think it's possible you're thinking with your dick instead of your head."

Reid froze. Coach was hitting a little too close to home with that one. "Just because I don't want to be a heartless bastard doesn't mean anything other than that, old man."

"Good. Glad to hear it." A heavy sigh came through from the other end of the line. "Look, son, you know I don't want to begrudge you any happiness. But this is it. You're getting up in age. If you lose this fight, it doesn't mean the end of your career. But it could mean the beginning of the end. You'll be given fights with the low men on the totem pole. And those kids are going to be younger and hungrier than you. Then once you've got a few losses under your belt, they'll stop giving you fights altogether."

"I know." Reid collapsed back onto the couch and let his head drop back. What concerned him was that the idea of his career coming to an end no longer terrified him as it once had.

"Then stay this next week if you want. But then you come back to camp and we'll make sure you're ready."

Reid still hated the idea of cutting his time short with Lucie, but the more he thought about it the more he realized it was better this way. She'd accomplished her goal, and with her help he was very close to realizing his. She'd worked miracles with his shoulder; it was almost at a hundred percent. And if he was this attached to her after only two weeks, it was bound to get much worse after another five or six. Yeah. This was definitely the way to go.

"I'll see you in a week."

. . .

"Honestly, I shouldn't have even tipped the guy," Stephen grumbled. "He was so busy falling all over himself for you that he barely did anything right the entire dinner."

Lucie stepped through the door he held for her, glad to feel the warm night air wrap around her and rid her of the chill from the air-conditioning. No matter how many times she froze in restaurants, she never remembered to bring a sweater.

"I think you're being too hard on him. I'm pretty sure he was a new waiter and still awkward at his job. It certainly didn't have anything to do with me."

"Well, no matter. Though the dinner itself left much to be desired, my company was easily five stars," he said as he lifted her hand to place a kiss on her knuckles.

It was a cheesy line with a cheesy old-fashioned gesture and the whole thing made her burst into laughter.

And snort.

Stephen's eyes widened and paused in his release of her hand like he wasn't sure if he'd heard correctly. She felt the color rise into her cheeks until she was sure her face was now an exact match to her dress.

"Sorry, I, uh," *Think, Lucie, think!* "I've been having some sinus issues recently."

Finally he moved, letting go of her hand and gesturing for her to start their short walk back to her apartment. As she fell into step, he said, "You should get that looked at. You don't want it to turn into sinusitis."

She wasn't sure how she should respond, so she opted for a subject change. "After years of working together in a professional capacity, it was so nice to finally spend some time with you on a more personal level, Stephen."

"I couldn't agree more. Although we didn't do a very good job at 'personal' over dinner, did we? We talked shop the whole time."

Lucie grinned, pleased she'd succeeded in directing the conversation the way she wanted. "Yes, I suppose we did."

"So, tell me about Lucie. What are your short-term and long-term goals, Ms. Miller?" Stephen sidestepped an empty slushie cup the size of a newborn lying next to a trash receptacle and continued walking.

Pausing long enough to pick it up and throw it away, she had to quick-step a few strides to catch back up to him since he hadn't noticed she'd fallen behind.

"Um, well, I guess my short-term goals would be things like getting some new equipment for the therapy room, taking some more classes on new techniques, and making an effort to get out more often."

He looked over at her. "Out more often?"

"Yeah, you know, *out*." When all he did was raise a questioning eyebrow she looked down at the sidewalk and tried to hide her smile of embarrassment. "As in dating."

Clasping his hands behind his back he said, "Ah, I see. Well, I hope you'll give me the chance to check that particular goal off your list."

Lucie spared a quick glance at him from under her lashes before refocusing on ensuring she didn't trip on anything. "I'd like that."

"Good. Okay, so what about the long-term goals? Where do you see yourself, say, in five years?"

She was starting to feel like she was on an interview, although she supposed that's what first dates were essentially. Considering she hadn't really been on any—with her only serious relationship they'd skipped over stereotypical dating by hanging out with his friends all the time—she couldn't really judge what was normal versus odd.

"Professionally I don't see myself doing anything different. I'm happy where I am."

"Really, you don't have any desire to move up? What about becoming the clinic director instead of just a therapist?"

"You mean take over for Annie?" She laughed as she pictured the scenario. "That woman runs a tighter ship than most naval captains. You've seen my office. If I took the helm, we'd go down faster than the *Titanic*."

He chuckled along with her for a few seconds, but then said, "Seriously though, why wouldn't you want to advance from where you're at now? I can't imagine being satisfied until I've gone as far as I can go in my field. I mean, why do you think I spend so many nights working on cases? It's not for the warm and fuzzy feeling I get from helping the patient."

Lucie snapped her head to the side. "You're not telling me you couldn't care less about your patients, are you?"

"Of course not," he said, putting his hands in his pockets. "I care about them. But I could care about them during my shift hours without working overtime. I do that part because I want to get ahead, get promoted. And if I have a truly special case one of these times, I can even write about it and get published in one of the medical journals.

"I do care about the people I operate on. I genuinely want to help them, or I wouldn't be a surgeon. But I don't see why it's a crime to care about me and my future, too."

Lucie frowned as she turned her attention to the cracks in the cement before her. She'd always known Stephen didn't work late on cases with her as an excuse to be in her company, but she'd thought for sure it was due to an immense dedication to their patients.

Then again, like he said, it wasn't that he *didn't* care about them. He was just conscientious about his career. He had goals, which last time she checked, was something to be admired. Giving him a reassuring smile, she said, "I understand. And I think it's great you have high aspirations."

As they stopped in front of her apartment building Stephen turned to her and put a foot up on the bottom stair. "We did it again."

She was suddenly so nervous about what might happen in the last few minutes of their date she couldn't follow his train of thought. "What did we do?"

He smiled wide. "We managed to bring the

conversation back around to work."

"Oh, that's okay, I don't mind. It's something we have in common, so it's natural our conversation leans in that direction. I think compatibility is important."

Stephen took a step toward her and her stomach dropped. He wasn't as tall as Reid so she didn't need to look up quite as far, and his leaner build didn't make her feel like she was being consumed by his mere presence, but the fact that his eyes had settled on her lips was enough to make her want to bolt for the door.

That wasn't right, was it? She should want him to kiss her. For years she'd dreamed of this moment. The moment he'd wrap his arms around her and the rest of the world would cease to exist as his lips finally met hers.

I'm just nervous. She'd built this moment up in her mind for so long she could scarcely comprehend it was here.

"Well, if this isn't perfect timing."

Lucie whipped around to see Reid walking toward them like a living ad for Nike's *Just Do It* campaign, wearing nothing but a pair of their black athletic pants and neon blue running shoes, hands on hips and breathing hard from a run. When he stopped a mere two feet away, the streetlamp above him highlighted the rivulets of sweat that trickled over the ridges of his torso before disappearing into the elastic riding low on his hips.

He extended his arm to her right to shake hands with her date. "Nice to see you again, Mann."

Though Lucie didn't move a muscle, she heard Stephen grasp Reid's palm and saw their arms pump up and down a few times in her peripheral vision. "Likewise, Andrews. I'm sorry we didn't get much of a chance to talk at the party the other night, but I'm always stretched thin at work functions."

"Understandable." They released each other, but Reid immediately pointed at Stephen's feet. "Careful, looks like you stepped in something there." In the two seconds it took for Stephen to be momentarily distracted, Reid leaned in and whispered in her ear, "You're looking to catch flies again, Lu."

She closed her mouth so hard she swore at least three of her molars cracked.

"I don't see anything," Stephen said as he straightened from his inspection.

"My bad. Must've been a shadow or something." Reid gave her a devil's grin and crossed his muscular arms over his chest. "So, you kids have fun?"

"We had a great time together, as always," Stephen answered from behind her. "Right, Lucie?"

"Oh, uh, absolutely," she said, nodding like a bobble head on the dash of an off-road vehicle. "Great time."

Dear God, he'd had to *prompt* her! Why had her brain decided to take a leave of absence *now* of all times? Stephen must think her an imbecile. Or worse, unconvincing. This was too much; she had to get out of there and into her nice, safe apartment. She turned her body a quarter turn so she could keep an eye on each of the threats facing her. "Oh, crap! I forgot I was supposed to feed Remy, Mrs. Egan's ferret, because she's... uh...visiting her sister."

"Ferret?" Stephen had obvious disappointment etched on his face. Reid simply arched a brow as if waiting for the rest of the story.

"Yes, ferret," she said. "You know, they're small, weasely creatures. I'm not that fond of them myself, but Mrs. Egan just adores the little rascal."

"I know what a ferret is, Lucie, and I'm sure it'll be fine for a while longer."

Before she could spit out another lie, Reid swept in as smooth as if they'd rehearsed the act. "Actually, no. Remy's diabetic so he needs to eat and receive insulin at strict times. I'd do it for her, but I'm severely allergic."

"Yes!" she said with too much enthusiasm. "Um, I mean, Reid's right, I really do have to go. But I had a really nice time, Stephen. Thank you so much."

The smile he gave her was strained around his eyes, but he was gracious enough to relent on the condition that he get to take her out again so they could discuss things of a more personal nature next time. After agreeing and receiving an awkward hug from him as Reid looked on, Lucie finally retreated to her safe haven to shower and lay in bed as she mulled a thousand things over in her mind.

Reid hadn't followed her in earlier, but she heard him come in several hours later. Knowing he was home and then listening to the sound of him taking a shower just down the hall was what finally allowed her mind to rest, and she fell into a wonderful dreamless sleep.

CHAPTER FOURTEEN

Thunder rumbled in the distance, seemingly louder for the empty streets upon which it echoed. "Reid, those storm clouds are ready to open up on us. Where are we going?"

Lucie had asked the same question no less than ten times in the last half hour and she wasn't getting any closer to an answer. He was remarkably tight-lipped about their destination and purpose for going there despite his obvious excitement. Dragging her behind him down a sidewalk in the artsy area of town, he kept glancing at her with a secretive smile that gave him a boyish charm and made her giggle like an equally young girl.

It had been a couple of days since her date with Stephen, and Reid had been extremely scarce other than during his training. Then

suddenly he announced he was taking her to
a late dinner and then to see something. She'd
thought maybe it was a show of some sort,
considering the part of town they'd driven to, but
by the time they'd left the restaurant it'd been
after eleven, so she was clueless.

"A summer storm never hurt anybody.
Almost there, come on," he said as he tugged her
into an alley.

She dug her heels in, causing him to pull up
short. "What could you possibly need to show me
in some dark alley?"

He stepped into her body and cupped the side
of her face with his free hand. His thumb traced
short strokes at the edge of her cheek. "Don't you
trust me, Lu?"

Staring into hazel eyes that melted her
insides with the heat swirling in their centers, she
whispered, "Of course I trust you."

Full lips spread into a smile. "Then close your
eyes."

She almost argued the need for such a thing,
but something about the way he looked at her had
her lashes lowering without hesitation.

A light kiss touched each of her lids as reward.

Reid led her down the alley another twenty
feet or so and then stopped. She heard what
sounded like keys entering a lock and a heavy

door creaking open. Once again he led her forward. She desperately wanted to open her eyes, but didn't want to ruin his surprise. Chewing on her lower lip, she waited while he closed the door and moved around the room doing things she couldn't discern by sound alone while telling her to keep her eyes closed.

Finally, he approached her from behind, wrapped one arm around her waist, and held his other hand over her still-closed eyes. "Shit, I'm starting to have second thoughts about this."

She could hear the anxiety in his voice. "Why would you have second thoughts?"

"Because I don't know what you're going to think. I'm worried you'll hate it."

Lucie canted her head to the side and repeated his earlier question. "Don't you trust me?"

• • •

The room was black as pitch with the exception of the overhead floodlight he'd turned on to shine directly over an easel, and on that easel sat a large cork-board holding a charcoal pencil drawing of Lucie...nude.

Don't you trust me?

Did he? Art was extremely personal and

something as intimate as this—the way she looked to him when they made love—was even more so. She had every right to be offended, even if they were the only people who would ever see it. It was still a liberty he'd taken without her permission.

He'd like to think he didn't know what had possessed him to do something as crazy as sketch a nude of Lucie, but he'd be lying to himself. Something about her—about the way he felt when he was with her—had resurrected his creative side from its years of slumber. Enough to where he'd called different art studios until he'd found a guy who'd been willing to let him use some space and supplies for a couple of days in exchange for some tickets to his upcoming fight.

And *this* was what he'd been inspired to create.

So whether he trusted her to receive it as the gift it was meant to be or not didn't really matter, because keeping it hidden from her like a dirty little secret was out of the question. There was no backing down now. *No guts, no glory.*

He took a deep breath, his chest expanding against her shoulders, then let it out slowly. "Okay," he said, lowering his hand. "Open your eyes."

Lucie gasped softly before covering her mouth with her fingers and whispering, "Oh, my

God."

Whether it was a good "Oh, my God" or a bad one, he couldn't yet tell. He hoped like hell it was the former.

Though he knew every stroke by heart, he studied the drawing and tried to view it through her eyes. Charcoal lines and curves depicted her on a chaise in the throes of passion, her back arched, her head turned to the side with hair spilling over the edge of the cushion. Her right leg hung off the couch, the ball of her foot planted on the floor for leverage. The other bent sharply at the knee, her toes pointed and raised several inches. Stretching down her body, her right hand disappeared between tight thighs, while her left hand reached across and caged her right breast, the turgid nipple peeking out between spread fingers.

His favorite part was her face.

Thick bangs partially covered her brow and the way it always furrowed when she experienced a burst of pleasure. With eyes closed, her eyelashes laid elegantly above slightly flushed cheeks in their wispy spikes. Her mouth was full, her kiss-swollen lips barely parted as though a gasp had just broken their seal. And the heart-shaped freckle sat at the corner of her eye. A tiny detail most people might not notice if it was missing, but to him it was the difference between it being any other woman and being *Lucie*.

He came back to himself when she took slow steps toward the canvas as though mesmerized. As she continued to take in the picture like she would at an art museum, he stood at the light's edge with his hands in the pockets of his jeans and did the same with her.

Tonight she'd donned a pretty, bright pink sundress with spaghetti straps. The bodice fit her like a glove, nipping in at her small waist and draping over the small flare of her hips with the flowy hem dancing at midthigh with every move she made.

"Reid, I…" She trailed off, and he feared the worst.

"What do you think? It's okay; you can tell me the truth."

She looked over her shoulder with tears in her eyes.

"It's magnificent. You're remarkably talented," she said, turning her attention back to the drawing. "You made me…" She took a deep breath and released it on a shaky exhale. "…beautiful."

His steps echoed in the sparse room as he crossed the few feet to turn her and hold her in his arms. One hand framed her face and wiped away a single tear that trickled over her cheek.

"That's where you're dead wrong, sweetheart. It took me several tries before I came even close to capturing your beauty."

She smiled wanly. "You're sweet to say so, but in a million years I could never look like that."

Lightning flashed through the room with a clap of thunder, and rain began striking a discordant song on the window behind him. The storm seemed to be escalating along with his frustration.

Reid wanted to choke every person who'd ever made this woman feel less than the incredible creature she was. Not only was she every bit as gorgeous as she was in his drawing, but everything about her—humor, awkwardness, klutziness, compassion, dedication—all of it, made her far superior to any woman he'd known.

He was about to tell her exactly that when she added, "I mean, come on. If I looked like *that*, I'd have Stephen wrapped around my little finger."

• • •

Temporary insanity. That was the only thing she could think of as to why she would say something so incredibly insensitive to Reid.

It didn't matter that half of their situation was her mission to end up with another man, and that he had no emotional stakes in their anomalous relationship. Reid had given her a special part of himself by creating this amazing work of art for her—*of* her—and she'd just slapped him in the face by bringing Stephen into their night by mentioning his name.

She saw the tempest of his anger roll across his eyes, the muscles in his jaw flexing several times as though trying to prevent himself from unleashing his thoughts that were no doubt things that would make her cringe, and yet nothing she wouldn't deserve.

"Reid, I'm so sorry, I—"

He didn't wait for the rest, but spun on his heel and slammed through the door into the storm outside. She chased after him, stopping just outside the studio to see him eating up the pavement toward the street, his suit shirt already half-soaked.

"Reid, wait, come back!"

He came to an abrupt halt, but didn't turn around. With hands fisted at his sides and his wide shoulders heaving, he looked feral and dangerous, and God help her, sexy. Shivers ran down her spine and goose bumps raised over the flesh of her arms, but it wasn't from the cool rain pelting her skin and drenching her hair. Even seething angry the man affected her on the basest of levels, and it both thrilled and frustrated her.

When he turned and stalked toward her with a menacing gleam in his eye, Lucie wondered if she shouldn't have let him walk it off and apologize later as he backed her up to the brick wall. She knew she should apologize again, should say something, *anything*, but words failed her as she stared up at a side of Reid she'd never seen. His demeanor was positively animalistic, and it sure as hell wasn't of the cute and cuddly kind.

"What is it about that asshole that has you so twisted up?" he shouted. "I'm serious, please tell me, because lately I've been trying to figure it out and I fucking can't!"

Twisted up? If she was twisted up over anyone, it was Reid. This was supposed to be a casual arrangement, nothing more than lessons on how to be the kind of woman who attracted a certain orthopedic surgeon so they could live happily ever after in her companionable relationship based on mutual interests and professional respect.

As it was now, she wasn't sure what she wanted anymore. Actually that was a lie. Her brain told her she wanted Stephen. But her body—and Lucie feared even her heart—was screaming for Reid.

She shook her head, sections of her hair

slapping against her cheeks. Hot tears spilled over and she prayed they blended in with the raindrops so she didn't look as pathetic as she felt. "I don't know what you want me to say."

The peak of his faux-hawk arrowed slightly over his forehead, heavy with the water streaming from its tip. His shirt, a pale gray with silver pin stripes he'd left open at the collar and cuffs rolled up over his muscled forearms, was now soaked through and plastered to his body.

He braced his hands on the wall by her head and leaned into her personal space a little more. He imprisoned her gaze with a stare so intense she was helpless to look away, and when he spoke, his words were razor-sharp. "Are you thinking of him when I'm inside you, Luce? Do you wish it was *his* cock buried inside of you instead of *mine*?"

She'd hurt him. More specifically, the softer side of him. The side that made him a thoughtful friend and considerate lover. The side that touched her body as though his fingers worshipped every curve, then transferred that reverence to canvas.

So now his fighter half was taking over, fortifying his defenses with harsh and crass questions in an effort to disguise his wounds. But though it might be the fighter's words pouring from his mouth, it was the artist's feelings behind them. For the first time, she truly understood the duality of his nature.

Lucie shoved all thoughts of what she needed aside and focused on what it was *he* needed. Confidence settled over her as she framed his face with her hands, the short stubble of his beard tickling her palms.

"Never." Surprise flickered in his eyes before his mask slipped back into place. "The moment you touch me, I lose myself to you, Reid." Stretching up on her toes she placed a kiss on his lips. "Every. Single. Time."

Thunder boomed overhead as a strobe of lightning cast his animalistic features in a pattern of shadows and highlights revealing his intent. She only had a moment to prepare and then his mouth descended quicker than a viper strike and just as deadly.

She moaned and opened to him, reveling in the hot swirls of his tongue as his hands palmed her ass and pulled her in hard against his rigid cock straining behind his zipper. Arching into him, she tried to obliterate every air molecule that separated them, needing as much contact with him as possible for fear she'd die without it.

He slipped a hand between them, moved her panties aside, and thrust two fingers deep inside.

She broke their kiss, unable to stop herself from crying out to the storm above as the sudden intrusion rocked her to her core.

"Goddamn it, Luce," he said gruffly. "I love that you're always so wet for me. I've never felt anything so tight and hot. I want to live inside of you and never leave."

Speech was impossible, so she made do with a pleading whimper and a roll of her hips to try and get him to move. It worked, but not how she'd meant it to. Instead of fingering her like she thought he'd planned, he pulled completely out and left her empty.

"Reid, please…"

"Don't worry, baby, it's only for a second." She watched as he ripped the fly of his jeans open and pushed them down enough to release his erection. Long and thick, ridged with veins and capped with the smooth, round head, she had a sudden desire to drop to her knees and take him in her mouth, but he didn't give her the chance.

Digging his fingers into the flesh of her cheeks, he hoisted her up, deftly moved her underwear aside, and drove himself in to the hilt. Lucie buried her face in his neck and clamped down on her bottom lip as darts of pleasure shot through her center. Immediately he retreated and thrust forward, setting a feverish pace that felt necessary for their survival.

The mineral scents of wet stone mixed with the floral scent of her drenched hair and the spicy cologne on Reid's shirt. The sounds of rumbling clouds and rain pelting the world around them wrapped them in an elemental cocoon and almost made her believe they were the only two people on earth.

His mouth ravaged her lips, her jawline, her throat, her shoulder. The tips of his fingers gripped at the edges of where he penetrated her, his large hands spreading her apart to allow him as deep as he could go.

She dug her nails into his nape, mimicking the bite of the bricks at her back. Rain streamed down their faces, yet they didn't blink as they stared into each other's eyes, connecting their souls as he connected their bodies. In a million years, she could never think of another man when she was with Reid. She wasn't capable of thinking at all when she was in his arms.

Everything melted away except this moment, this man who had the power to consume her until nothing mattered but the way he filled her, stretched her…completed her.

All too fast she felt her climax bearing down on her. She didn't want this to end. She wanted it to go on forever. Clenching her teeth, she tried to hold it back, but it kept building and building.

"Let it go, baby. I want to feel you squeezing my cock. Come for me," he growled.

In another half a dozen strokes his teeth clamped down where her neck met her shoulder and she lost her last thread of control. They came together in a cataclysmic explosion. He roared like the feral beast he'd become in the dark alley as he spilled his hot seed into her clenching sex.

Lucie shattered into a million pieces, dancing in the thunderous clouds above for a time before falling with the rain back to earth...back to Reid.

When they'd caught their breath, he gently lowered her to the ground, keeping his arms around her until he was sure her legs would hold. He cupped her cheek, kissed her lips, and said, "Let's go home and get you out of the rain, hmm?"

She gave him a small smile and nodded. "What about the drawing? It'll get ruined in the rain."

"We can leave it here and pick it up another day. Come on. I'll get you into a hot shower and then into bed."

She arched a saucy eyebrow in his direction. "You didn't get enough just now?"

Grinning he said, "I don't think I could ever get enough of you, Lucie, but no, that's not what

I meant. I want to take you back, take care of you, and tuck you into your warm bed so I can hold you until the sun comes up."

"Oh." A sarcastic retort. A perverted line. An unsavory joke. Any of those things would've been the response she expected from him. But never something that made her insides turn to complete mush.

He locked the studio, kissed the top of her head, and tucked her into his side as they made their way back to the car.

Was it possible to physically feel the moment you lost your heart to someone? Because Lucie was fairly sure she'd just lost hers, and the spot where it should have been literally hurt.

CHAPTER FIFTEEN

"Thanks, Fritz. Run me a tab will ya?"

The man winked in response before attending the next bar patron as Lucie grabbed the large glasses of beer and carried them to the booth in the back corner of the room. Vanessa was on her cell, arguing with someone as usual.

"Absolutely not. I don't care what they're offering, we're not settling. Look, I'm entering a very important meeting right now so I'll call you tomorrow. Uh-huh, buh-bye." Tossing her wild curls over a shoulder she dropped her phone unceremoniously into her purse with a dramatic exhale of relief as they performed their habitual clinking of drinks and toast to their health. "So what's up? You haven't called an EDM since you were freaked out about finals senior year."

True. Usually Vanessa was the one calling for

an Emergency Drinks Meeting due to her latest drama, whether personal or professional. She had a flair for melodrama, which made her amazing to watch in a courtroom, but it also meant she was either riding the highs life had to offer or drowning in the inevitable lows. Lucie had always been the even-keeled one. Yet another way they balanced each other out.

Lucie took another drink to bolster her courage and then voiced her problem aloud for the first time since it had wormed its way into her head. "I think I'm falling for Reid."

Her friend let out an obnoxious whoop like she'd just won a few hundred bucks on a scratch-off she expected to be worth nothing. "I thought you said something was wrong, but this is awesome! Congratulations, honey, he is one fine male specimen. Mm-mm-mm. What's he like in bed? I bet he's fantastic, right? Damn! I want every last detail, including length, girth, and if it hooks to the side."

"For the love of God, will you please lower your voice?" Lucie hissed. "I am *not* giving you any details of his anatomy."

Cue gigantic, pleading kitty-cat eyes. "Don't make me beg, Lucie. The men in this town aren't even worth the effort to tear the foil wrapper off a condom, much less talk about the disappointment afterward. You have to tell me what it's like to ride a stallion like him."

Lucie clapped a hand over her nose and mouth until she'd successfully swallowed her beer without choking on it. "What makes you even think we had sex?"

"Now you're insulting my intelligence."

She snorted. "More like your freaky sixth sense."

Vanessa shrugged. "Tomato, tomahto. C'mon, give me *some*thing."

Glancing around to make sure no one was eavesdropping she said, "Yeah, okay. We've…"

"Screwed like rabbits?"

"Been intimate," Lucie said with a quelling look. "And it was…"

"Phenomenal, out of this world, good enough to make you instantly bend over and grab your ankles every time he looks at you?"

Lucie stared with mouth open and eyes wide. "That was a little over the top, even for you, Nessie."

"Sorry, I got carried away. Continue."

"It was wonderful."

Vanessa screwed up her face like she'd just swallowed stale beer. "Wonderful? You can't come up with a better adjective than wonderful?"

Lucie gazed at the ceiling in thought for a

moment, then back at the crestfallen woman across from her. "Nope. It really was wonderful, in the true sense of the word."

"Okay, fine, I get it. I need to wait till you're drunk before I'll get any of the good stuff out of you." Lucie laughed and thanked Fritz's daughter when she brought their next round just as they were finishing the others. "So why is it a bad thing you're falling for Reid? I must be missing something because I don't see any evidence to support that theory."

"What do you mean?"

"Well, I've only hung out with the guy a couple of times, but we both know I'm an excellent judge of character. The guy is full of win." Holding up her left hand she started ticking off character traits on her fingers. "Insanely attractive, funny, charming, rich, insanely attractive, successful, friends with your brother, and he obviously carries a torch for you. Did I mention insanely attractive?"

"No, I don't think so," she said wryly. "And what's with the torch thing? It sounds like something my grandmother would've said."

Vanessa rolled her eyes. "First I'm too lewd for you, now I'm too prim. Fine, the guy obviously has a hard-on for you. Is that better?"

"Yeah, that's perfect. Just what I want is a guy

who likes me for a little easy side action."

"That's not what I meant," she said, her green eyes softening. "I see how he looks at you. He's totally into you. Like, *really* into you. In fact, I wouldn't be surprised if he—"

Lucie held her hand up. "Don't. Don't say it because he doesn't. It's not like that for him."

"How do you know?"

Leaning back against the high back of the booth she met her friend's determined stare. "Come on, Nessie, you're not my mother. You don't need to soothe my ego. Men like Reid Andrews don't fall for girls like me."

"Why is it so hard for you to believe you're worthy of a good man's love? You're the most beautiful person I know, inside *and* out. He'd be a fool not to fall for you."

Lucie lifted her glass and took several large swallows. Could Vanessa be right? Could Reid really have feelings for her? She thought back over the last few weeks, her mind cataloging things into columns. Things a friend would do versus things a lover would do. The lover column was filling up fast with the friend column sitting pathetically low. Butterflies took flight deep in her belly as she looked up to see a smug grin on Nessie's face.

She shook her head. "Even if you're right,

how can it work? We're total opposites. I've done that before, remember?"

"No," she said leaning forward for emphasis, "what you did was get involved with a jackass who didn't truly love anyone but himself. The relationship failed because the douchebag couldn't keep his dick in his pants, Lucie, not because he liked saving cows and you liked eating them."

"Amen, Red!" Fritz slammed down a fresh round of beers and braced his fists on the table. "I never could stand that pansy-ass, tree-huggin' nancy." He shook a thick, arthritic finger at both of them as he spoke. "Never trust a man if he don't at least drink beer. A man that only drinks things ending in 'tini' ain't really a man. He might as well be announcing the size of his pecker as he is ordering a drink, if you know what I'm gettin' at."

The girls laughed and thanked him for the sound advice, assuring him they'd hold every man to that wisdom from now on.

"Well, all right then. This one's on me, long as you gimme some sugar." The old man leaned down so they could each plant a loud, smacking kiss on his cheeks covered in white stubble. Standing up he said, "Now that's a perfect way to end the night. I'mma let Michelle close up tonight and head on upstairs. You gals behave, y'hear?"

After they promised and bid him goodnight, Lucie turned to Vanessa with equal parts excitement, terror, and determination. "Okay, tell me what to do."

Vanessa's green eyes seemed to literally spark with mischief and a corner of her mouth hitched up. "He's been giving you seduction lessons, right?"

"Yeah," Lucie answered warily.

"So it's simple." Vanessa placed her arms on the table in front of her and leaned in. "You go home, put those lessons to good use, and show the teacher just how good of a student you really are."

•••

Reid pulled the door open to his old gym and walked through slowly. The tangle of emotions brought on by the familiar smells and sounds transported him to an earlier time. A time when he was young and under his father's thumb.

"What the hell's the matter with you? For the last goddamn time, *get your hands up*!"

The echo of his father's voice in the large, open space acted like an overdose of lactic acid in his muscles, causing tension and pain. He followed the sound of mumbled gripes to a ring where it looked like a high school kid was sparring with a guy who could've been the center of a college football team.

"Watch his take down! He's gonna go for—" The bigger guy shot at the kid's lower body, wrapped his arms around his hips, and tackled him to the mat. Stan Andrews called a time out and the fighters broke apart, one sucking in labored breaths, the other looking bored. "For fuck's sake, Peterson, why do I even bother with you?"

"Sorry, Coach," the kid said, lowering his eyes to the mat.

"Still busting balls I see," Reid said through a tight jaw.

His old man's head didn't move much, but his eyes cut over and narrowed on his only son like he was sizing up an enemy before he finally straightened, crossing his arms over his chest. "Well, well, if it ain't the prodigal son."

"It's been a while since you've read the Bible, Pop. The prodigal son returns home after leading a misguided life and begs for his father's forgiveness. I'm not returning. Just visiting. And all I've ever done was lead the life you trained me for so I have no reason to apologize."

"Oh, you don't, do you? How about apologizing for taking everything I gave you—all the knowledge, all the training, all the dedication—and leaving me behind while you live your big life in the big leagues."

"I didn't leave you behind," Reid argued. "I offered for you to come live out there with me. I have a large guesthouse you can have all to yourself. You turned it down."

Stan scoffed. "Live out there as what? A retired has-been fighter living off his son's charity? No thanks. I shoulda been your manager."

Reid worked his jaw and repeated a calming mantra in his head several times before allowing himself to speak again. "Look, I didn't come here to argue. I was in the area and thought I'd say hi—talk—but if you're too busy that's fine, too."

After a minute or two of staring at each other, his dad finally showed signs of life. "Peterson. Grady. Hit the bags for a while. You," he said pointing at Reid, "come with me."

Reid followed his dad into the small office consisting of a worn metal desk and a couple of folding chairs in front of it. Stan sat behind the desk in the beat-up vinyl chair sporting several strips of silver duct tape to hold torn edges together. Reid spun one of the chairs around and straddled it, laying his forearms on the back. Everything in him told him to get up and leave. He knew he wasn't going to get any warm and fuzzies from his father. At least, that's how things would've gone years ago. Maybe his father had softened over the years.

Yeah, and maybe his mom would walk through the door and say how she hadn't meant to leave them like a pair of shoes she no longer cared about.

One of the things his father had taught Reid was to analyze people's body language. If you paid attention to that—whether in a fight or out of one—you could almost always anticipate your opponent's next move or how they'd react to yours.

The older man leaned back in the chair and folded his arms over his barrel chest. He was guarded and unhappy about his son's surprise visit. "So why're you here? I'm sure you're not looking for any pointers with all them fancy trainers you have back in Vegas. You come to gloat about your success?"

"Geez, Pop, can't you just drop your resentment of life for one fucking minute?" When all he did was scoff, Reid took a deep breath and tried for civil. "I have a fight coming up. It's a title fight to win my belt back from Diaz."

"Yeah. I know all about it." Stan gestured toward Reid's arm. "Shoulder healed?"

The fact that his father knew about his fight

and his injury shouldn't surprise him. Being an active coach, it only made sense that he still followed the sport. But damn if that little kid inside of Reid didn't swell with pride at knowing his dad was up-to-date on his life. Stupid kid.

"Yeah, almost a hundred percent. I've been working with a really great PT. She's worked fucking miracles with it. Actually, you know who she is. Lucie, Jackson Maris's little sister. Remember her?"

Reid was taking a chance bringing up the Maris family for any reason with his father. Since Reid had spent any spare time he had at Jackson's house, the relationship between the adults had been strained to say the least.

His dad stroked the stubble on his jaw with one hand as he thought back. Then he grunted. "Quiet little thing. Kinda gangly and awkward if memory serves."

"Not anymore," Reid said with a half smile. "She's gorgeous, not to mention totally amazing. But, yeah, that's the one."

Stan leaned forward, his eyes narrowing. "You fucking love her or something?"

"No, it's not like that. I mean, yeah, I really care for her—" Reid cursed on an exhale. "I was thinking about maybe trying to do the whole relationship thing. See where it leads."

Stan jabbed a finger in his direction. "Now you listen to me, boy. You might be in the twilight of your career, but I'll be damned if you haven't managed to stay on top with as old as you are. You'd be a fucking idiot to throw that away for a woman."

Reid stared his old man down and kept his jaw clenched tight to avoid yelling and causing a scene. "I'm not throwing anything away. There are plenty of guys that manage to have relationships while having careers in the UFC. Some are even married."

"And how many of those"—he actually paused to make air quotes around the next word—"*relationships* actually last? I'll tell you right now, there's only two kinds of women out there. The kind that love the lifestyle, the publicity, the traveling. It's what they crave and it offsets all the shit they have to put up with to have it. But as soon as it's gone, so are they.

"Then you have the kind of woman who won't put up with the life. They might at first, and they'll tell themselves that it'll get better and the relationship is worth the sacrifices. But eventually they realize they deserve better than what we can give 'em, and then they're gone, too."

Reid stood up and pushed the chair out of his way. "Look, just because your wife left you, doesn't mean the rest of the world is doomed to the same fate. Lucie isn't like that."

Stan slapped his hands on the desk as he rose, stormed around, and got right in Reid's face. "That's what you think! You *think* you know someone. Love them with everything you have and then they decide they're better off without you and they leave. That's reality, kid! So don't go thinking you're fucking special and the rules don't apply to you."

Reid's temper flared and he raised his voice to match. "Think I'm *special*? Where the hell would I ever get a stupid idea like that? Sure as fuck wouldn't be from you. You never let me forget I was only as good as my next win."

"That's because it's the truth! We're fighters, Reid! It's who we are, what defines us."

Reid lost the battle with controlling himself and let his emotions run. Yelling back, just like in his younger years, he said, "I love fighting, but being a fighter is *not* the only thing I am! It's *not* all I'm good at!"

"Oh really?" Stan's voice finally leveled out, but just because he wasn't yelling didn't make his response any less acrimonious. "I suppose you're referring to your silly sketches and sculpting now. That's just what every woman wants is a grown man who plays with clay all fucking day. Gimme a break."

Old feelings of inadequacy bubbled to the surface, threatening to choke the breath from his body. Reid knew he'd gotten past all of his dad's bullshit years ago, but for whatever reason, when it came to dealing with his old man, Reid felt like that insecure kid all over again.

His dad cursed, sank into the vinyl desk chair again, and dragged both hands down his tired-looking face. "You do what you want. It's your life. But if you came to get my advice, here it is: You've got life by the balls, kid. You've got fame, fortune, and you can get laid all you want without any attachments. Keep it that way...and spare yourself the heartache."

Reid scoffed and opened the office door, shaking his head. He'd known this visit wouldn't go well, but his conscience wouldn't let him blow off his old man regardless. Sometimes he wished his conscience was like the grasshopper from *Pinocchio*. That way when it caused him to do stupid shit like this, he could squash it under his heel.

"Thanks for the pep talk, Pop," he tossed over his shoulder on his way out. "As always, it's been a pleasure."

CHAPTER SIXTEEN

Reid strode into the apartment and made a beeline to the fridge. He grabbed two bottles of beer, downed the first in seconds, and then cracked the second one open as he headed onto the balcony.

Since the place was dark, he figured Lucie was still at the bar with Vanessa, which was perfect because his mind was a jumble of things and he needed time to straighten it all out. He took a giant swig of the cold liquid and wished it could cool his emotions from the inside. Maybe he'd break his diet for one night and get stone drunk. Numb himself for a few hours so he didn't have to think about his upcoming fight or the fact that he had to leave Lucie in a few short days.

Hell, he hadn't even told her yet. Every time he tried his gut tightened and he ended up kissing her instead. And that sure as shit never led to a conversation. Not one of words anyway.

Lucie.

What the hell was he going to do about her? He'd never felt for any woman even a fraction of what he felt for her. He loved being *with* her, and he certainly loved her as a person...then again he could say the same for Butch, but what he felt for her was a hell of a lot stronger than that of his trainer. But as far as being *in* love with her? Reid had no idea how he was supposed to know that.

He frowned and took another drink of his beer. Stone drunk was definitely starting to sound better and better.

"You look way too serious for a beautiful night like this."

Startled, he spun around, ready to berate her for sneaking up on him...when he got a look at the sexiest fucking thing he'd ever seen.

She stood in the open doorway to the balcony, hands braced on either side of the doorjamb, and one leg cocked up on the ball of her foot. Until that moment, if asked what he thought the sexiest thing a woman could wear would be, he would've said see-through lingerie.

But Lucie in nothing but one of his dress shirts that covered her from shoulders to midthigh blew away anything she could've picked from

Victoria's Secret. Her hair was loose and full like he'd already plowed his fingers through it, and she had a sparkle in those silvery eyes that spoke volumes.

"Speaking of beautiful," he rasped.

She began to back away slowly, but beckoned him to follow with a crook of her finger. Draining the last of his beer, he reentered the apartment and closed the sliding glass door without taking his eyes from her. When she disappeared around the corner toward the bedrooms he set his empty bottle on the table, kicked his sport sandals off, and strode down the hall until he found her standing in front of her bed.

Just before he crossed the threshold, she held out her palm and said, "Wait," effectively stopping him in his tracks. "You can come in here on one condition."

He flexed and fisted his hands, trying to control his instinct to pounce. "And what's that?"

"You do as I say. The minute you break my rules, everything stops."

A slow smile stretched across his face. She was trying her hand at seduction. He inclined his head. "I agree." *For now*, he added mentally.

"Then come here and kiss me."

One slow, deliberate step at a time he stalked her, trying to see if he could get the upper hand right away with intimidation. He had no intention of making her first attempt at control a cakewalk. He was going to test her. Push her. See if she could keep him in line. Oh yeah, he thought as he reached her, this was going to be fun.

He slid a hand to her nape and wrapped his other arm around her middle just before he took her mouth. And man did he take it. Fisting her hair, he angled her head and thrust his tongue inside and consumed her. Her body melted into his and he wondered if her foray into the land of seduction wasn't already over.

No sooner had the thought taken wing when she pushed on his chest enough to break his hold on her. They stared at each other, chests heaving with shallow breaths. Her ruby lips, properly swollen from his kiss, beckoned. She was mere inches away, and he wanted her so damn bad. The fighter in him yanked on the chains of restraint he'd agreed to, wanting to take back the upper hand, take back the control.

And yet he waited.

Waited until those bee-stung lips spread into the sexiest wicked smile. One that promised him rewards of the most lascivious kind, which just so happened to be his favorite. Maybe patience was a virtue after all.

She walked him around until his back was

to the bed. Grabbing the hem of his T-shirt, she slowly pulled it up his body. Her knuckles barely grazed his skin and yet it felt like they shot bolts of electricity straight to his balls. Once she divested him of his shirt she laid her hands on his shoulders and moved them over every inch of his torso, her fingers undulating over the ridges of his muscles as if committing them to memory.

Next they worked on his belt and the fly of his jeans. He'd been halfway hard just from seeing her in his shirt and kissing her senseless, but with her hands so close and the anticipation of events to come, it was now fully on board and straining to get out.

As she dragged his jeans down his legs, she knelt on the floor sending erotic snapshots to his brain of all sorts of possibilities with her in that position. Once his jeans were gone, her hands ran back up his thighs and her gaze raised to his. Her mouth was so close to his cock he could feel the warmth of her breath seep through the cotton of his boxer briefs, making him harder than he ever thought possible.

Her eyes never left his as she dragged her lower lip up the length of him and then used her teeth to lightly graze over the head. He growled in the back of his throat and his dick jerked in response. "Ah, fuck. You're killing me," he ground out.

She smiled up at him, clearly proud of herself, as well she should be. Either she was a natural who'd come out of her shell, or he was a better teacher than he thought.

Her fingers hooked his underwear and a second later he was standing before her, completely naked, his hard-on jutting out from his body to point directly at what it wanted. Her normally soft gray eyes were like molten silver, burning him as they visually groped his erection.

Lightly, she used the tips of her fingers to explore its contours from root to tip. The glide of her skin and soft graze of her nails as they trailed across the swollen head of his cock drove him to near insanity. Instinctually Reid's hands wrapped themselves in her hair, ready to guide her sweet mouth over him.

"No," she said firmly. "Grab the bedposts."

He gave her a wry smile as he followed her orders. He'd forgotten who was supposed to be in charge. Force of habit.

"Keep your hands there. If you move them, I stop whatever I'm doing and back away."

When she raised her eyebrows as though to ask if he understood the consequence of disobeying, he nodded. Then added a silent prayer that he not explode the moment her lips finally touched him for the first time.

Settling back on her feet, she wrapped one delicate hand around the base of his cock, angling it down to her mouth. A drop of precum seeped from the tip. If he'd thought she'd be hesitant or shy about something so visceral, he'd have been wrong. Instead, a hunger gleamed in her storm-gray eyes as she lapped up the bead in one long lick. He hissed in a breath, the feel of her silken tongue combined with seeing her—not just any woman, but *his* woman—on her knees in front of him rating as the most erotic thing he'd ever experienced.

At last she opened that sweet mouth of hers and encased him as far as she could go, her tongue swirling and massaging, her cheeks hollowing from the suction she made with her ruby lips with every retreat before sinking over him again.

The next minutes shattered into fragments of eternity as she worked him over with the sweetest kind of torture. Her hot mouth and sinful tongue had all six hundred and forty of his muscles strung tight as a bow. At one point he feared snapping her bedposts in half, but was unable to relinquish his white-knuckle hold for fear she'd stop and he'd lose what little sanity he had left.

The ecstasy she gave him was like someone dropping a match into a room full of fireworks. It started with only one or two little flares, but those in turn set off the ones next to them, and so on and so on, until his entire body felt like a fucking Fourth of July finale.

His climax hit him so fast and hard that he had no chance of warning her. He tried to do the gentlemanly thing and pull back, but she grabbed his ass and dug her fingers in as she swallowed him deep. Any polite inclinations he'd had went up in smoke with the bite of her nails in his flesh and, throwing his head back and his hips forward, he roared as he came until she'd taken every little bit he had to give.

As the stars disappeared from his vision, Lucie stood and backed away slowly, running her fingers over the open throat of the shirt she wore.

"What are you up to now, woman?"

"I took care of you." She sat demurely on the upholstered bench for the vanity that sat directly across from her bed. "Now I'm going to take care of me."

"I believe that's my privilege," he said, releasing the posts.

Before he could advance she ticked a finger back and forth. "Ah-ah-ah. Be a good boy and stay right where you are."

"Boy?" he scoffed. "Let me come over there and I'll show you just how much of a man I really am, sweetheart."

She undid the lowest button on the shirt. Then the next, revealing her blue silk panties. She gave him a wicked smile and said, "If you want to prove to me just how much of a man you are, then you'll fight the instincts gnawing at you and stay right. Where. You. Are."

Fucking smart. Now if he moved he was branding himself a pussy. And all because he wanted *hers* more than he wanted to breathe in that moment. When this was over he was telling her in no uncertain terms that he'd be the one doing the seducing from now on. As hot as it was to watch her in this role, he was too much of a control freak when it came to sex. After this, he'd be calling the shots during their hot interludes. He could hardly wait.

Then it hit him. There wasn't much time left to make love to her. Depending on their schedules they'd have a few more times together, tops. The realization hit him like a blow to the solar plexus, damn near knocking the wind right out of him.

Don't think of that right now. He didn't want anything to taint what precious time he did have with her. He was going to make every second count until the final bell rang.

"As you wish, princess."

Another button was released, as was a warm

laugh. "I love that movie. So now you're my farm boy, is that it?" He waggled a brow in answer making her chuckle again, but then she cocked her head to the side and sobered again. "You know, as cute and heroic as Wesley is, I can't bring myself to pretend you're anyone else." The last button holding the shirt together slipped through its hole and the sides fell open to reveal her perfect breasts. "You, Reid Andrews, are exactly who I want."

Although his brain tried to tell him she only meant here and now—because it wasn't a secret who she truly wanted for the long haul—he couldn't stop his heart from leaping in his chest.

"That's good, Luce. 'Cause you're exactly who I want, too." *Now, and every day after that.*

Shit, he had to stop thinking like that. He had to stop thinking period and give himself over to the moment. To the woman he had *in* this moment.

"Mmm," she moaned as she tweaked her nipples between her thumbs and forefingers. "How much?"

His eyes were glued to her breasts as she continued to stroke and fondle them. "How much what?" he croaked.

She leaned back against the wall. One hand slid down her flat stomach to her pussy and rubbed over the thin, blue material. "How much do you want me?"

Reid's entire body vibrated with the effort it took to keep himself locked in place. His hands fisted with the itch to touch her satiny skin. His mouth watered at the thought of sucking on the taut peaks of her breasts and lapping at the cream between her legs.

Pulling the panties to the side, she used her other hand to massage the supple lips of her pussy, slipping a finger between them to delve into the wetness. She looked like something out of his wet dreams. Ass perched on the edge of the seat and leaning back with her shoulders pressed to the wall. His shirt open and barely clinging to her shoulders with her hair spilling on either side of her neck. And her slender legs were spread wide, raised on the balls of her feet, while her fingers explored his promised land.

"Bad." His voice was pitched lower than usual and he noticed it sounded more than a little growly. The woman brought out his animalistic side like no other.

Her middle finger slid deep inside, her eyes closed and back arched as it swirled around. When she removed it her body relaxed once more and her eyelids fluttered open. Then she pinned him with a sultry stare as she brought that finger up to her mouth and painted her lower lip with her juices.

He heard a loud groan and it took him a second to realize it had come from him.

"How bad?" she asked before licking her lip with the tip of her raspberry tongue.

"So goddamn bad it hurts." Reid glanced down at his cock already strained to its limits so soon after she'd made him come with her mouth, then looked back up at her. "Literally."

A seductive smile spread over her face. "Then come and get me, hotshot."

He moved as fast as he did in the octagon, making the feet between them seem like mere inches. His hands delved into her hair on either side of her face and he hunched over to conquer her mouth and suck the remnants of what she'd left on her lips.

Their kiss wasn't slow or tender, but deep and fierce, constantly changing angles as they devoured each other.

Eventually he wrenched his mouth from hers to kneel between her legs. He dragged his hands down her body until they reached her perfect breasts where they molded and kneaded and pinched her ripened nipples, making her writhe on the bench and her breaths quicken.

"You're so fucking beautiful," he said, just

before he closed his mouth around a hardened peak and drew on it hard.

She cried out and grabbed his head, her nails scratching his scalp through his short hair, trying to pull him in even more. He placed his hands along her spine, holding her to him so she didn't accidentally squirm away. Switching from one to the other, he kissed them as he did her mouth, tongue lashing, teeth grazing, lips sucking.

"Oh, God, Reid…"

Her stomach was pressed along his chest with her legs hooked onto his back just under his arms. And in between, her hips ground that hot pussy on his abs, searching for the means to an orgasm.

He kissed his way up her body, reveling in the wanton sounds of his woman. Placing one last kiss over her heart, he lifted his head to find her staring at him with The Look—the one that told a guy when a woman was leaving Let's Screw For Fun City and headed straight for Let's Pick Out China Town—written all over her pretty face.

Normally The Look had him making up forgotten urgent appointments and sprinting in the other direction. He tucked her hair behind one ear and studied her for several moments, waiting for the familiar flight response to kick in. But all he felt was the need to gather her closer. The need to make love to her until muscle exhaustion forced them to rest.

It was in that moment Reid knew even if he had an actual appointment, he'd blow it off to stay with Lucie. It was in that moment, he knew he loved her.

"Reid?" she said softly. "You're looking at me funny."

"Am I?"

She nodded.

He removed her shirt and panties, then cradled her in his arms as he stood and made his way over to her bed. Once she was settled in the middle of the mattress he climbed next to her and propped his head on one hand while the other drew lazy patterns over her body. "Funny how?"

"I'm not sure. I've never seen that look on you before."

Her breaths grew more shallow and her nipples puckered into tight little buds as he trailed a finger around the soft curves of her breasts. "I doubt anyone ever has...but you're not just anyone, are you?" He kissed her shoulder and raised his eyes to find a slight frown of her brow and her lower lip prisoner between her teeth. "You're special. You know that, don't you, Lucie?"

She smiled and nodded.

She was lying.

Her smile was one of the saddest he'd ever

seen, and it killed him that she still had insecurities. Insecurities that had no business gripping a woman as wonderful as her.

Reid took it as a personal affront. One he intended to rectify.

. . .

Earlier, as she'd waited anxiously for him to return home, Lucie had made a decision. No more would she ignore what was in front of her because of a silly compatibility theory based on a failed relationship. It was time to be honest with herself—to be honest with *him*—and embrace her true feelings for the man who knew her as no other ever had.

And that time was now.

Reid studied her with an intensity she'd never known. His eyes, rings of mossy green infused with streaks of topaz, bore into hers. Her gut instinct was to look away, to guard herself not only against him, but against what she felt for him. It was because of that instinct that she held firm… and let him in.

Lucie trembled lightly as she lay there, her heart and soul exposed to a man with the power to crush them. There was no denying she loved him, not when she felt this vulnerable, this afraid.

The callused tips of his fingers grazed her cheek before delving into her hair. His face was only inches away from hers and yet it might as well have been miles.

"Baby, you're shaking," he whispered.

"No, I'm not."

He smiled as he nuzzled her cheek with his nose and kissed her jaw. "Yeah, you are. Don't worry…I'm going to take care of you."

Before her brain got on the hamster wheel about whether he was referring to the next sixty minutes or the next sixty years, he claimed her lips in the most sensual kiss of the century and killed any hope of brain activity for the immediate future.

His lips moved over hers, exploring the curves and contours, his teeth nibbling, testing the fullness of her lower lip, and his tongue traced the inner arc of the upper one. Every time her tongue ventured forward, he pulled back, not allowing her to participate to that degree. Over and over she tried to kiss him back, but he expertly avoided her attempts while continuing his explorations.

Frustration and sexual tension mounted deep in her center. Her hands grabbed his head to hold him in place and she was rewarded with a deep kiss. She moaned, tasting herself on his tongue. Before Reid she'd never known how good it could be to have a man worship her sex with his mouth. And she never imagined how much she would love kissing him afterward.

Lucie's small victory didn't last long. After a few brief moments he grasped her wrists and pinned them to the mattress above her head as he moved over her. His hips settled in the cradle of her thighs, his thick erection nestling between her folds.

He bent his head to kiss her neck and lick a path to her ear. He nipped her earlobe then sucked it into his mouth to soothe the pain away. Releasing it, he spoke, his hot breath feathering through her hair. "Lucie, baby, you drive me insane, you know that? You have no idea the control it's taking me to keep myself from driving into you like a complete madman."

She arched her body, encouraging him. "Don't hold back. Take me," she begged.

Pushing himself up just enough to look her in the eyes, he said, "Oh, I will. But this time I'm going to savor every moment. I'm going to take my time loving you tonight."

Lucie opened her mouth to argue when he shifted his hips, sliding his cock up until its hard length rubbed over her clit, and her argument changed to a high-pitched moan.

"No talking allowed. Just feeling." He repeated

the move, causing her to see stars. "Got it?"

She nodded. She'd agree to anything so long as he kept doing that.

Reid kissed his way down her body, leaving moist trails over her breasts, down her rib cage, and across her stomach. His hands pushed her thighs wide, opening her as far as possible. She gazed down her body at his head poised just above her pelvis, his breaths skating over her wet skin and sending shivers of pleasure that hardened her nipples.

This time he kept his eyes open, lending another level of intimacy to the act as he hit her with that first long lick up her center.

She sucked in a breath, and her hips jerked.

"One of my favorite things is taking you to the edge," he said, his voice low and gravelly. "The way you look just before you come is a thing of pure beauty."

Another lap of his tongue with a flick at the top over her clit.

"Oh!"

"That's it, baby. Keep watching me. Watch me make love to you with my mouth."

Those were the last words he spoke before making good on his intention. Reid licked and sucked like he was kissing her mouth, his tongue diving into her, humming his appreciation of her taste.

She panted and fisted her hands in the comforter. Her hips began to thrust instinctually against his tongue, needing a consistent movement over her clit to match the pulsing deep inside getting faster and faster.

"Oh, God, I need you inside me," she cried. "Reid, please!"

"Not yet," he said in a voice that sounded as strained as she felt frustrated. "The edge. You're not there yet."

Was he joking? She bloody well *felt* like she was there. If she didn't get something inside of her in the next few seconds, she was going to lose it.

He replaced his tongue with two fingers, rapidly rubbing over the sensitive bundle of nerves as he sucked at her lips and bit her inner thigh. The sheen of sweat now covering her body and the scent of her arousal hanging thick in the air confirmed his oral talents. He was driving her batshit insane and enjoying every second of it.

She released the comforter in favor of stimulating her nipples and squeezing her breasts. She'd always been too self-conscious to play with herself before, but the urge to touch them was too great. The tweaks she gave her nipples zinged straight to her center, and the tension in her belly tightened more and more.

Lucie's vision became unfocused, but she heard Reid growl, "Fucking beautiful" as he moved back up and entered her body just as she reached that edge and then shot past it.

Unable to help herself, she screamed and arched against him as her insides imploded and bore down on the massive erection now blessedly filling her to capacity. He groaned against her neck and tightened his arms around her as her channel continued to spasm and wave after wave of tingly vibrations spread through her body to the tips of her toes and the roots of her hair.

"Goddamn, you feel amazing."

She would've agreed, but even the simplest speech seemed beyond her. As she came back to herself, wrapped in a euphoria she'd never known existed, Reid's mouth captured hers in a sweet, languid kiss.

Losing herself in the heady post-climax fog and the sensual dance of their tongues, her body jerked in response when he began to withdraw, the thickness of his shaft rubbing along the sensitive walls of her sex.

Once he was almost fully unseated, he pressed back in, slow and deliberate, until she'd taken all of him again. She gasped and arched her head back, breaking the kiss. The sensations were too much, too soon. She'd never survive.

She placed her hands on his shoulders and pushed with the strength of a baby bird, her eyes pleading with him. "Reid, I can't…"

"Shh," he said against her lips. "Yes, you can." He pulled her hands away, entwined their fingers, and held them down just above her head as he withdrew again. Holding himself still at her entrance, he whispered, "Trust me."

It wasn't a statement of arrogance, or even a request. Staring into the fathomless depths of his light eyes, Lucie realized it was a plea. It said, *Trust me to pleasure you. Trust me to take care of you.* And dare she hope, *Trust me to love you.*

"I trust you."

His lips crushed her in a molten kiss as he drove himself to the hilt. She had a fleeting thought that this must be the very definition of pleasure-pain, wanting to push him away and claw him closer all at the same time.

But it only took moments before ecstasy had her firmly in its grasp and all that mattered was the exquisite feel of him moving steadily inside her, completing her as nothing else could.

Time stood still, the turning of the world ceasing in deference to their love making so it could last forever. Their bodies, slick with sweat, moved as one, as fluid as the rolling swells of the ocean tide.

His torturous, unhurried pace finally broke, his hips driving faster, their breaths growing shorter. Soon the familiar tension began to gather deep in her center, growing and spreading with every thrust of his cock until his passion consumed her, owned her.

Unbelievably she came yet again, his name spilling from her lips. But whereas the last one had pulsed with fierce intensity, this one carried her into a perfect oblivion on a seemingly endless current.

"God...*Lucie*," he cried, his muscles tensing and quivering with his release. And as he poured himself into her body, she imagined him pouring his love into her heart as well.

CHAPTER SEVENTEEN

Reid held a sleeping Lucie against his body and willed himself to remember every detail. How she fit perfectly in the crook of his shoulder. How, in the middle of the night, she hiked her leg all the way over his hips as though she was afraid he'd somehow escape if she didn't. The way her hair draped over his arm and her hand rested lightly over his heart.

They'd made love and talked for hours last night, exploring each other in ways he'd never done with anyone else. Even after realizing he loved her, he'd known his time with her was limited, but he decided to let his fantasy play out in the shadows of the night. He'd wanted to stay awake, to take advantage of every second he had with her, but eventually they fell asleep in the early predawn hours. Now the morning sun streamed through the bedroom window, chasing away the fantasy and leaving him with the ugliness of reality.

"Hey there."

The scratchy sound of her morning voice made his heart skip a beat. But when she lifted her head from his chest with an impish smile, it might have stopped altogether.

She rested her chin on the top of her hand and seemed content to watch him. Those long, spiky lashes hung at half-mast and her lips were swollen from sleep, or maybe still from his kisses and bites mere hours ago. Her dark hair was tousled and even looked snarled in some places, but it framed her face beautifully.

"Hey there, yourself. Did you sleep well?"

Her smile went from imp to Cheshire cat. "Incredibly well." She inched up and placed a tender kiss on his lips before snuggling back into his side and groaning. "Can we take the day off and stay in bed?"

She couldn't have had a better request to drive home the fact that he didn't live by normal standards where the occasional day playing hooky was okay. He shut his eyes and placed a kiss on the top of her head, giving her one last squeeze before letting her go and getting out of bed.

Retrieving his jeans and yanking them on, he

said, "Sorry, sweetheart, but I don't get days off, and we slept in pretty late already."

"Ugh, I suppose you're right. Okay, here's the plan," she said, crossing to the bathroom. "You go for your run and by the time you get back I'll have already done my yoga, downed the necessary amounts of caffeine to make it through the day, and made my phone call."

Reid picked up his shirt and looked over to the open bathroom door, where he heard the water running in the sink. "What phone call?"

She emerged from the bathroom in a short robe, brushing her teeth and smiling. Pausing long enough to speak with a mouthful of toothpaste she said, "I have to cancel my date tonight with Stephen before I forget. Can you imagine if he showed up and *then* I canceled?" Then she added in a fun singsongy voice, "Awk-warrrrd," as she returned to the bathroom.

He indulged in the idea of her calling off her date with Mann...But only a selfish asshole wouldn't want the woman he loves to be happy, even if it couldn't be with him. *Shit.* Clearing his throat he prepared to say the hardest three words he'd ever spoken.

"You shouldn't cancel."

She poked her head around the half-open door, her brows creased in a frown. She pulled the toothbrush from her mouth again. "What do you mean I—" Light blue foam dripped down her chin. "—ick. Hold on."

When she ducked back in to spit and rinse he caught a glimpse of himself in the dresser mirror and almost threw a punch to shatter his reflection.

"What do you mean I shouldn't cancel?"

He turned to see her standing several feet away, holding her arms across her chest as though trying to give herself a supportive hug. She was preparing to hear what he suspected that loser ex of hers had said to her. Preparing to get hurt all over again.

Reid swore a hot knife plunged deep into his gut when he looked into those big, dove-gray eyes of hers. He couldn't do it. He couldn't have this discussion yet. Hell, he wasn't even sure what kind of discussion it needed to be. He had to get out and clear his head, a.s.a.p.

Crossing to her in just a couple of strides, he placed a chaste kiss on her forehead and did his best to sound upbeat. "I just feel bad for the guy is all. I mean, only one date and then dumped on the day of the second?" Reid put his hand over his heart. "As a fellow dude, let me just say, 'Ouch.' Eating dinner with the man a second time just seems like a small price to pay to prevent an ugly suicide."

She did a combo chuckle-snort that made his heart ache, and then pushed at his chest playfully. "You're too much. Go for your run and we'll talk when you get back," she said before heading for the kitchen.

Reid blew out a big breath. Disaster averted… for now.

He changed into his running gear and was pounding the pavement in record time. The heat of the midmorning scorched his body as he pushed it harder than usual. The rhythm of his shoes striking the ground wasn't meditative for him today, but instead felt like a countdown on a ticking time bomb. Counting down the seconds until he had to present Lucie with his decision.

The idea of leaving her made his stomach turn and his muscles knot up.

Before he'd gone to see his dad he'd been toying with the idea of asking her to come back to Vegas with him. And although he knew his dad was just a bitter old man with a narrow point of view, Reid couldn't discredit everything he'd said.

Lucie definitely didn't fit the description of the kind of woman who loved the lifestyle of a fighter. His mom had fit into that category, but not Lucie. She liked her somewhat small city and being one of the few PTs in the area, which gave her the opportunity to really get to know her patients. And even though she was one of the most disorganized people he'd ever met, he'd come to learn that she liked routine. She liked knowing what to expect and when to expect it. Trying new things and spontaneity—two things Reid took incredible pride in—were not easy for her.

Uprooting her to Vegas would be a huge culture shock for her. Sure, she'd be able to get herself on a routine like she was here, but the routine would include almost never seeing him when he was preparing for a fight. He spent the majority of his time training, cutting weight, and studying how to beat his next opponent. There was little time left in his daily routine other than falling into bed, only to get up at the crack of dawn the next morning to do it all over again.

And then there was the traveling, the publicity. The bullshit stories the tabloids printed. All of it was a bitch on relationships. He'd seen it happen with several of the guys. The stress caused fights, and the women turned bitter, resenting the sport that consumed all their men's time, and eventually, the men themselves.

It would kill him to see Lucie's sweet disposition turn into something jaded and resentful, all because he couldn't stand the idea of living without her. Just because she was perfect for him, didn't mean he even came close to being right for her.

She deserved so much more. She deserved to come first not only in a man's heart, but in his life. Someone who could take the occasional day off just to lie in bed with her, who had a successful career that didn't involve the possibility of getting concussed or choked out.

Someone so very not *him*.

As he rounded the last corner to the apartment he slowed to a walk, procrastinating as much as possible. He anchored his hands on his hips and drew in deep breaths as if they could cleanse him of the sickness taking root in his gut. But with every step he took it only grew worse. He'd be lucky if he made it through his shower without dry heaving over the toilet.

For the first time in his life, Reid was dreading a fight.

· · ·

Lucie sat at her kitchen table, head resting on one hand while the other drummed the theme song to *The Lone Ranger* while waiting for Reid to emerge from his bedroom.

After his run he'd given her a halfhearted wave on his way to the shower, and now he'd been in his room for at least twenty minutes, which was about eighteen minutes too long to change into a pair of shorts and T-shirt. So now she was, of course, paranoid. It seemed being in love had turned her into a neurotic teenager. Yippee.

Finally she heard the door down the hall open. Picking up her pen, she pretended to concentrate on the Sudoku puzzle in front of her that she'd randomly written numbers on. Thank goodness they'd never discussed math puzzles or he'd know she was full of shit. She couldn't do one of those correctly if her life hung in the balance.

When she pretended not to realize he stood in the doorway of the kitchen—she'd die before she let him know how crazy his absence made her— he cleared his throat.

She looked up from the newspaper with a smile…that died when she saw the bag in his hand and the look on his face.

"What's going on?"

"I got a call from Butch. Scotty's back, so he wants me to come back to camp to finish my training before the Diaz fight."

"Oh." Ignoring the twinge of slightly crushed pride from the insinuation that she couldn't do as good of a job as the other guy, she looked at the situation logically. "Well, that's good. It's important you get back to your normal routine and people."

"It has nothing to do with your capabilities, Lu. You're an excellent PT. You've already worked miracles with my shoulder. I couldn't have been this successful this quickly with anyone else. I mean it."

"Thank you." *Pride: soothed.* She offered him a warm smile. "I understand, really. And since I still have the vacation time, I can finally see Vegas!"

"I don't think that's such a hot idea. I'm not going to have time to be with you like I had here. It's a totally different ballgame there. I won't be able to take you around. You'd be stuck in my place all day, every day."

Something was wrong. Was he really that worried that she'd be upset he wouldn't have the time to entertain her? "That's okay. I can go sightseeing by myself during the day."

He brushed a hand forward over his hair and dragged it down his face. "I'll be too tired at night to spend any time with you, Lucie. It'll be like not seeing me at all."

No. No, no, no. He was *not* doing what she thought he was doing. She stood up and crossed her arms, narrowing her eyes in warning. "What the hell is really going on here, Reid? You're trying awfully hard to get me to stay home. With really lame excuses, I might add."

"Look, please don't make this any harder. You know I care for you, but this"—he pointed back and forth to each of them a couple of times— "was only temporary. Remember?"

"Remember? Yeah, Reid, I remember. I also *remember* last night when all of that changed. You're not honestly going to stand there and deny that, are you?"

He didn't say anything for several minutes— seconds? Hell, it could've been an hour, she didn't know—with nothing moving on him except the ticking of the muscles in his jaw. So he was aggravated. Big flipping deal. She was about to go nuclear.

At last he cut through the silence with words that could've been samurai swords for as sharp as they were. "Last night was great. Just like all the other nights. But the arrangement is over now. You wanted Mann to notice you and be interested—which he has, and he is—fulfilling my part of the bargain. Your part of the bargain to get me healed in time to fight for my championship belt has also been fulfilled. So that's that."

"No that's *not* that! You're running away like a damn coward, *that's* what this is. Not any bullshit excuse about following the terms of our so-called deal." Adrenaline buzzed through her veins, making her slightly light-headed, but she just grabbed onto a wooden chair for balance and pressed on. "Things changed between us, Reid. You know it, and I know it."

"I'll admit things went from clinical to personal, but it would've been impossible for it not to. Sex with someone you care about is personal. But that's not enough to base a long-term relationship on, you know that."

Their voices were rising, and somewhere in the back of Lucie's mind was the warning that much louder and she'd have Mrs. Egan knocking on her door. Or worse, calling her brother. But she didn't care.

"What about *love*, you big dumb jerk? Isn't that enough? Because I do. I am totally and utterly in love with you!"

The world fell silent. Not even the ticking of the clock on the wall dared make a sound as the two of them stared at each other. Maybe time had stopped. Maybe this was one of those moments where an angel would suddenly appear to give her sage advice or the chance to rewind life a couple of minutes so she could take back the words that made her more vulnerable than she'd ever been in her life.

His eyes were strangely cold, much like she imagined they looked as he stared down an opponent before the ref called for the fight to begin. She'd never seen them like that before, and they were killing her. Then he spoke and she realized she was wrong...

"You loved your ex-husband, too, Luce. Look what that got you."

...it wasn't his eyes that ended up killing her after all. It was his words.

"Get out," she managed around the lump in her throat. She blinked, trying to keep the hot tears at bay. "I don't want to see you ever again."

No apology. No hesitation. He spun on his heel and six steps later was out of her life. For good.

CHAPTER EIGHTEEN

Weeks, not years. Reid had to remind himself it had only been a few weeks since he'd walked out of Lucie's apartment. It felt like a lifetime ago. Sometimes, when he was alone at night, lying in his California king—which now seemed obnoxiously empty after loving the way Lucie wrapped herself around him in her smaller queen—he wondered if he hadn't dreamed the whole thing.

But then he'd remember their last night together. The way she responded to him as he made love to her slow and gentle like he'd never done with any other woman. Like he'd never do again with any other woman.

Their month together had been all too real... and now his life without her was all too empty.

As soon as he returned to Vegas, he'd fallen

into his usual routine of training sessions mixed in with some specialized PT sessions with Scotty. Though the man was an excellent doctor and Reid's shoulder was as close to perfect as he could get it before the big fight, he'd practically had to gag himself so he didn't verbally compare everything Scotty did against Lucie's techniques.

He thought about her constantly, and he caught himself mentioning her practically every time he opened his big mouth. It got to the point where he decided it was safer to rely on nonverbal communication like grunts. Hell, it had worked for cavemen, why not him?

It was the day before the fight. Physically, he was golden. He was in great shape, his shoulder was decent, and at the weigh-ins earlier that day he registered at a perfect two-oh-five.

Mentally, however, he'd never felt more fucked up. Normally this close to a fight the only thing running through his mind were mental images of him overtaking his opponent. But the only image running through his mind now was the stricken look on Lucie's face when he purposely ripped the heart from her chest.

Reid growled, his frustration quickly escalating to pure anger, until he was yelling like a battle-ready Spartan. He picked up a medicine ball next to his feet and hurled it across the gym at the wall where a couple of his teammates stood next to his imaginary target.

"Whoa!" Brian said as he pushed off the wall. "What the fuck is your problem, Andrews?"

The right thing to do was apologize and walk it off. Too bad his Right Thing-ometer was irreparably damaged. "Maybe it's you, Harty," he said as he got in the man's face.

"Or maybe you're pissed off 'cause you're too much of a pussy to go after the girl you keep talking about till you're blue in the balls."

Reid's brain went on instant standby mode as his body took over. The last thing he remembered was seeing red and shooting in at his friend's hips, taking him down to the mats with a mighty roar to match the sound of the blood pumping in his ears. The next thing he knew there were arms everywhere peeling him off Brian and men shouting different things all at once so he couldn't decipher anything.

"That's enough! Break it up and hit the showers before I add a few more hours of cardio to drain the piss and vinegar outta ya's."

Butch. Finally a voice of reason. Reid shook off the last few hands holding him and went to gather his things.

"Andrews! In my office, now."

Reid spun on his heel and glared at his coach.

"I don't need a lecture. Cool my heels. Got it, message received. I'm going home."

"Hey! I don't give a good goddamn what message you received. Get your ass in my office."

Clenching his hands and grinding his teeth, Reid stalked into the coach's office and dropped into one of the guest chairs. Butch followed him in, closed the door and sat in the chair next to him, leaning forward with forearms on his knees.

"What's eatin' you, son?"

"I don't know what you're talking about," Reid said as he crossed his arms. When all the old man did was stare at him, he threw an arm out in the direction of the gym. "I'm trying to focus on my fight and they wanna bust my balls about shit. They know better than that, Coach."

"I saw what happened. You nearly took Harty's head off with a medicine ball."

Reid turned his head away, unable to look into the sky-blue eyes of the older man. He knew he'd acted like an ass—and he'd apologize to Brian later—but he didn't know what to say.

"Reid." The tone Butch used told him he'd wait there all day until Reid gave him what he wanted. With a resigned exhale he turned his attention back to his coach. "When you came back from Reno I was impressed with your physical condition. I was worried that without your normal routine you'd let yourself get soft around the middle, but ya did good and came back to us healthy as a horse and strong as an ox.

"But mentally—" Butch shook his head and tsked a few times. "Mentally you came back with a few screws loose, and I have a strong suspicion it has to do with that lady PT you were with. Am I right?"

Reid didn't know how to respond or where to start. So he didn't.

"Okay, fine. I'll tell you what I think," Butch said, leaning back with arms folded over his chest. "You fell in love with the Miller girl, but decided you weren't good enough for her, so instead of telling her how you felt you probably said or did something to screw it up just before coming back here. How close am I?"

Pushing to his feet, Reid dragged his still-taped hands over his face then hooked them behind his neck. "Dead on."

"I thought as much," Butch said, rising from his chair. "So what's your plan?"

Reid dropped his arms and narrowed an eye at his coach. "What makes you think I have a plan?"

"You never go up against a fight or a problem without a plan." Butch eased a hip onto his desk and popped one of the peppermint candies he'd replaced cigarettes with into his mouth. "But if the way you've been acting is any indication, your plan sucks."

"What the fuck is that supposed to mean?"

"Just what I said. When you have faith in your plans you're no different than you are any other day. Our plan for the fight is solid. But you're still messed up. Ergo—"

Reid lifted an eyebrow. "Did you really just say 'ergo'?"

"Yeah, I did, smartass—ergo, your plan sucks."

Reid couldn't argue with the man's logic. He was right. When Reid had a good plan, nothing fazed him. Not the head games his opponent flung at him through the media, not an injury he knew could be dealt with after the fight, nothing.

"My plan sucks because I don't have one. No matter how I try, I can't find a solution that makes us happy together."

Butch rubbed his jaw as he thought about… well, whatever it was he was thinking about. "Hmm. Yeah, I can see how that would trouble you."

Reid stepped to the interior office window and looked out at all the things that had been a part of his life for as long as he could remember. A ring for sparring, mats for grappling, padded dummies, punching bags, weights, and cardio machines. A feeling of indifference settled in the center of his chest like a crushing weight. He'd noticed that a lot lately upon entering the gym. Not even the familiar smells and sounds brought on the usual excitement.

He shrugged, feeling the tension knots in his shoulders. "It is what it is, Butch. Lucie isn't cut out for this life. If I bring her into it, she'll only end up leaving. She deserves someone better than me. Better than a fighter."

"Ah, Christ." Butch returned to his chair from earlier and gestured to the one Reid had first occupied. "Have a seat." Too tired to argue, Reid did as he was told. "Now I want you to listen and listen good. I'm sure you know this already, but I've never said it outright, so here it is: You know me and Martha couldn't have any kids of our own. Hell, it's why she's a schoolteacher and I decided to take on young men like yourself.

"Now I care for all my fighters—if I didn't, they'd be out on their asses looking for a new coach—but you've been with me a long time, and you're like a son to me. And no son of *mine* would have such a fucked up self-image. That's your old man talkin' through you, is what that is, and it's a bunch of bullshit."

"Butch, before I showed up she was half in love with an orthopedic surgeon. The guy took her on a date and wanted to take her on more. He's got money, good looks, and has a shitload of things in common with her."

"So?"

"So I'm already going in as the underdog! In the grand scheme of what women look for in a guy, Dr. Douchebag wins hands down."

"On paper. He only wins on paper, kid." Butch leaned forward and smiled. "What have I always told you the trump card is in any fight?"

Reid met the steady gaze of his coach and started to see a glimmer of light at the end of that long, dark tunnel he'd been in for weeks. "Heart. Any fighter can win against any odds if he has more heart than his opponent."

Butch slapped him on the shoulder and sat back with a satisfied smirk. "Exactly. And not only do you have heart, son, I'd wager you've got hers, too, if you want it. But that's up to you. Now, go home and get some rest. No matter what you decide you still have a fight tomorrow and I need your head on straight or you're gonna get it knocked off. Understand?"

"Yes, sir," he replied as he got up to leave. Just as he opened the office door his coach called his name.

"No matter what happens, I'm here for you. Good luck, son."

It seemed like such a normal sentiment. One that a person would hear any number of times in their life. And yet, that had been the first time Reid had ever heard those words.

He tried to speak—even a muttered "thanks" would've been acceptable—but his throat had completely closed up, not to mention his eyes were starting to water. Before he completely broke down he gave his coach a curt nod and closed the door behind him.

• • •

Reid straddled a chair with his wrists propped on the back as Scotty wrapped the athletic tape around his hands and fingers, preparing him for his fight with Diaz.

He'd had all night and most of the day to figure out what he was going to do about the situation with Lucie. A couple of hours ago he made a decision. A decision he couldn't have predicted a few months ago, but one he was surprisingly at peace with.

A knock sounded on the door and Scotty looked to Reid for direction. Some fighters hated any type of distraction before a fight. Reid had never been the kind who needed to drown out the world with music blasting in his ears as he jumped around the room, psyching himself up. He was more like a snake hiding in the grass. Quiet, patient, and introspective until the cage door closed behind him and it was time to strike.

Reid nodded at Scotty, who then called for the person to enter.

Assuming it was one of his teammates wanting to hang out in the room with him, he didn't look up. But at the first sound of the man's voice, Reid's head snapped up to see his father standing in the doorway, wringing his gray plaid cabbie hat in his hands.

"Hey," Stan said before clearing his throat. "I don't mean to bother you, but I just wanted to let you know I was here, so…"

Scotty ripped the roll of tape off and secured the end with a few hard pats. "You're all set, Andrews. You've got about a half hour or so." Glancing at Reid's dad, he added, "I'll tell your corner team to wait for you out in the hall."

"Thanks, Scotty." He waited for the door to close again before standing and addressing the man who hadn't come to one of his professional fights before. "Why're you here, Pop?"

"Look, if you want me to go—"

"That's not what I said. I just want to know… why now?"

Stan's defensive attitude leaked out of him,

his shoulders rounding forward slightly, his eyes dropping to the hat dying a torturous death in his grizzled hands. After a few moments, the older man sighed, rubbed a hand over the back of his head, and met Reid's gaze.

"When your mother left, I felt like she ripped the heart from my chest and took it with her. I made up my mind that I'd never love anyone ever again. And I guess that included you." With heavy feet he walked over to one of the couches in the room and sat down. "I was so goddamn angry at her, and looking at you was like…"

He shook his head as if to tell himself not to finish that thought, but it was pretty obvious what he'd been about to say. "I guess I thought if I was hard enough on you that you'd prove my theory right and give up…just like she gave up on us."

Reid straddled the chair he'd been in earlier again, afraid that without its support, he'd collapse from shock. Never in his life had he thought he'd ever have this conversation with his father. Though he'd always suspected the cause of his father's actions, to hear it directly from him was almost surreal.

Strength seeped into his father's stocky frame, and with his jaw set and his brown eyes locked onto Reid, his resolve was palpable. "But no matter what I did, you never quit. And I respect the hell out of you for that."

Reid refused to acknowledge the stinging behind his eyes, but it was much harder to discount the cracking of the ice that had entombed his feelings for his dad for so many years. "Guess I take after my father in that respect."

His dad swallowed thickly and blinked a few times until the moisture that had momentarily covered his eyes was no longer there. Then he stood and placed his now-wrinkled cap on his head. "Maybe the next time you're in town, we can go grab a beer or something."

A social outing with his dad? The mere idea was baffling. When he didn't answer right away, the man strode toward the door saying, "Or not, whatever. It was just an idea—"

Reid quickly swung himself off the chair. "I'd like that."

Stan pulled up just short of the door and looked back with something that almost resembled relief, but then covered it with a stiff nod in Reid's direction. "Good luck tonight."

"Thanks, Pop."

Reid wasn't sure how long he'd been standing alone in the room after his father had walked out, but it must have been a while because his teammates actually had to come in and tell him it was time to glove up and go.

Thinking he must have slipped into some sort of daydreaming twilight zone, Reid turned to one of his buddies and said, "Punch me." When all he got was a raised eyebrow in response, Reid slapped his stomach with both hands. "Come on!"

The guy shrugged and nailed him a good one right to the abs. He'd been ready for it, but Adam had a sledgehammer for a fist so it still pushed the air from his lungs. *Nope. Definitely not dreaming.* Rubbing his stomach, Reid grunted, "Thanks. I think."

"Anytime, man. You ready to do this?"

Reid nodded and accepted the red gloves held out to him. As he made his way down the long hall toward the arena and the roar of the crowd, Reid felt like he'd already won one fight tonight. His dad had extended an olive branch of sorts and said he was proud of him. Un-fucking-believable.

Now all that was left was to get through the fight with Diaz and go talk to Lucie. Sounded simple enough, but they were both going to be the fight of his life in their own way. One, he could stand to lose. A loss on the other would crush him utterly and completely, leaving him broken.

But like his dad said, Reid had never been a quitter, and his wins practically eclipsed his losses. So he'd do what he always did. He'd fight like his life depended on it. Because this time, it very well might.

CHAPTER NINETEEN

The ballroom resembled a starlit winter night in the middle of August. The committee had certainly outdone themselves, Lucie noted. Thousands of tiny lights twinkled among yards and yards of white tulle draped in graceful arcs along the ceiling with dozens of white paper lanterns hung in the spaces the netted lights had left open.

Tables were draped in linens, topped with fine china, and surrounded by linen-covered chairs; all in white. Even the floral arrangements in the center of the tables and placed around the room were white roses, cut to several inches from the bloom and placed in shallow glass bowls until the entire surface area was filled. No greenery necessary.

The only colors in the entire room were the

dresses of the guests. Moving among the white backdrop they sparkled like gemstones of every color, with the exception of the men in their black tuxes. Lucie watched them congregate and move in packs and almost shot punch from her nose when she realized they looked like penguins waddling on the ice of the Antarctic.

"Are you okay?" Vanessa asked as she patted Lucie on the back. "I told you not to drink the red punch when you're wearing a white dress. It's too risky. You should be drinking club soda or water."

Lucie set the punch on the table in front of her and glanced down at her floor-length satin sheath dress with a sigh. Next year she'd have to make friends with someone on the decorations committee so she wouldn't end up looking like part of the furnishings. Good thing she'd picked up a bit of color at the beach last weekend so at least she was visible above the strapless bodice. Still, she felt indistinguishable from her snow-white surroundings, blending in where others shined.

And wasn't that just a metaphor for her life.

She looked over at her best friend who'd been kind enough to come as her date since Lucie had purchased two tickets a month ago with the hope of bringing Reid. Vanessa was of course radiant with her wild red-gold hair tamed in a French twist and an emerald gown that looked dyed to match the exact shade of her eyes. She drew the attention of every man in the room effortlessly. Ever the yin to her yang.

"Remind me again why you couldn't just use my ticket and bring one of the guys from the firm with you?" Lucie asked as she scanned the room dejectedly.

"Ah. That, my dear, is because you have an inherent inability to say 'no' to people and agreed to be put up for auction like a piece of meat," she said a little too cheerfully.

"Oh right. That."

At the mention of the Date-A-Doc Auction Lucie's stomach performed acrobatics worthy of an Olympic Gold. The auction—where guests at the ball could bid on members of the hospital staff for a date—was always the biggest fundraiser of the entire event. Lucie had never been asked to participate before, nor had she wanted to be. Unfortunately, one of the female residents came down with mono the week before and Sandy, the head nurse who embodied every depiction of Mrs. Claus ever known, begged Lucie to take her place.

The sound of a microphone clicking on and being tapped a few times poured from the large speakers at the head of the room where a stage had been erected for the event. "Can I have everyone's attention?"

Speak of the devil.

A jovial Sandy in a lovely pale blue gown stood center stage with the auction program in hand.

"Oh, God," Lucie muttered while holding a hand to her stomach.

"Come on," Vanessa said, grabbing her by the hand. "Let's go find Kyle and Eric, hold up the bar, and get you well and properly buzzed on clear alcohol until your number's up."

"Until my number's up?" she repeated, incredulous, then relaxed and rolled her eyes. "Oh, you mean until it's my turn."

"Duh-uh," Vanessa said with a giggle.

"Actually, what you said is a rather appropriate turn of phrase considering how I feel. Lead the way, oh, wise one."

For the next half hour Vanessa and the guys stood with Lucie and watched as men and women were called up one by one to the stage and asked to stand there as a short bio was read of their interests and hobbies like a cheesy rendition of *Love Connection.*

All night Lucie had managed to steer clear of Stephen. After Reid had broken her heart and solidified her theory that incompatible couples were doomed, she'd gone on one more date with him. Though she knew it was more out of spite than still believing she loved the handsome surgeon, she'd done her best to note his good qualities to prove that she could be at the very least content with him as a partner in marriage and life, should things go that far.

But by the end of the night, all she'd managed was comparing every little thing he did or said to Reid. And as she expected, Stephen fell woefully short on every level. She'd even let him kiss her at the end, hoping that a spark of chemistry would make up for other areas where he lacked. But it had only proved that kissing Stephen Mann was as exciting as pressing her lips to a CPR mannequin, which had also reminded her that her certification was due for a re-up. So at least it hadn't been a total loss.

Despite how badly it hurt, Lucie couldn't bring herself to regret falling in love with Reid. The few weeks they'd spent together had been the best weeks of her life. He'd taught her so much about herself and how to live life instead of simply watching from the sidelines. She was more confident, more comfortable in her own skin, and she owed that all to him.

So after a full week of crying into countless pints of Cherry Garcia ice cream—and a home intervention by Nessie and the boys—she'd picked herself up, brushed herself off, and looked to the future with her head held high.

Her biggest problem now was that she and Stephen had done a complete role reversal. After that date she'd told him that it just wasn't going to work out. He countered with ideas of grandeur of what their life could be like and asked her on another date. To the hospital ball. The very thing she'd wanted from the beginning.

And now she was at the ball, alone, and wishing she was curled up in her apartment with the one person she'd been certain was all wrong for her.

Yep, she thought as she downed the last of her drink. Her life was now the very definition of irony.

"Last but not least we have a wonderful young lady who stepped in at the last minute when Stacy fell ill, Miss Lucinda Miller. Come on up, dear."

The crowd applauded the calling of their final victim. Lucie pinned a glare on Eric and Kyle and poked each of them in the chest discreetly. With a fake smile plastered on her face she said, "If one of you aren't the highest bidders, I will personally see that you're both eunuchs by the end of the night."

"Yes, ma'am," they answered together, glasses

raised and all smiles.

She mentally scoffed as she made her way to the stage. They weren't taking her seriously, but they'd better come through. They'd promised they'd make sure no one else won her. That way she did her part, the hospital got money, and she didn't have to go on a date with anyone creepy, crotchety, or any other bad words that started with a "cr" blend.

Several minutes later, she stood next to Sandy as she finished reading a bio Lucie couldn't even remember writing. And then it began.

"Okay," Sandy said into the mic, "let's start the bids at five hundred dollars."

"Five hundred," Kyle said from over by the bar.

Sandy gestured in his direction. "Excellent! Can I get seven fifty? Seven fifty?

From the left corner of her eye Lucie saw a man raise his hand. "Seven fifty."

Stephen. "Ah fuck." Lucie froze and barely refrained from slapping a hand over her mouth. She couldn't believe she'd said that out loud! Damn alcohol loosened her bar tongue at a fancy event. Wonderful.

Sandy moved the microphone away from her mouth and whispered, "I'm sorry, dear, did you say something?"

"Um, I said 'what luck.'" Lucie gave her what

she hoped was a sheepish grin. "I was afraid I wouldn't get any takers."

"Nonsense, honey, you're a beautiful young woman." Then she returned to her role as auctioneer and raised the price to a cool grand.

For the next several minutes she watched anxiously as her price kept getting higher and higher, driven up by Stephen's bottomless checkbook. Lucie had assured the guys she'd pay anything over their budget, but in her wildest imagination she hadn't thought Stephen would hang on this long.

The bid was now up to twenty grand, and it was Stephen's. Lucie made eye contact with Kyle and gave a slight shake of her head as Sandy asked for another five hundred from him. Going on another date with the man wasn't the end of the world. It certainly wasn't worth putting herself and her friends in the poorhouse over.

But if she were being completely honest with herself, it was less about going on a third pointless date with Stephen, and more about the date being a painful reminder of what she would never have with Reid.

Sandy perked up beside her, "Okay then, twenty thousand going once...twenty thousand going—"

"One hundred thousand," called a deep voice

from the back of the room. A voice Lucie knew as intimately as her own.

Gasps and whispers filled the hall and the crowd twisted in their chairs in almost perfect unison. Reid stepped farther into the room until he came to stand in the center of the tables. All eyes were on him, and yet his were trained fully on hers and never once waivered.

On some subconscious level, Lucie knew she was staring wide-eyed and stunned like a deer in headlights, but she'd never seen anyone so sexy before in her life. Reid stood out like a giant among men. The tuxedo hugged his large frame perfectly, no doubt because it had been tailored to do so, unlike most of the men who probably rented their ill-fitting outfits.

He was perfection personified. She drank in the sight of his bad-boy looks that set him even further apart from the sea of average males surrounding him. Suntanned skin and the pointed tips of his tribal tattoo snaking up his neck stood out against the stark white of his shirt. A shirt that lay open at the throat, his bow tie hanging loose around the collar like he'd been in too much of a hurry to do himself up properly.

His hair was styled in the barely there faux-hawk she loved, and the trimmed growth of his beard made her miss having whisker rash in delicate places. His bottom lip sported a healing cut and an angry red abrasion highlighted one of his cheekbones giving his refined look a feral edge.

But it was the way his hazel eyes bore straight through to her soul that awakened the butterflies in her stomach to fan the embers of her desire that had her knees weakening.

Sandy cleared her throat and practically squeaked, "I beg your pardon?"

"I bid one hundred thousand dollars, for one date, with the stunningly beautiful woman on stage." Then he turned his head to pin Stephen with a challenging glare. "Unless of course someone raises the bid, in which case, I'll raise mine as well."

Lucie bit her lip while she waited for Stephen's reaction. After several moments of looking between her and Reid, he finally shook his head. Lucie blew out the breath that had been burning her lungs as Sandy announced Reid the highest bidder. It was either that or the woman just found out she won a trip to Disney World. It was hard to tell with the excitable, high-pitched, mile-a-minute way she was talking.

Whatever the cause for Sandy's excitement, Lucie wasn't paying attention. Her eyes were glued to the devilishly handsome man walking toward the stage as the band struck up their first song of the evening.

When he reached the bottom of the stairs, he held out his hand. Her body moved without encouragement from her brain, as if the simple act of holding out his hand affected her with a gravitational pull she had no hope of fighting.

But she preferred to think of it as avoiding a scene if she were to throw a drink in his face, which is what she really wanted to do. Right? Of course right.

The moment her hand slipped into his, an almost imperceptible tingling sensation traveled up her arm and spread through the whole of her body. Without speaking a word, he led her onto the dance floor where couples started to gather. He pulled her into his body, fitting her against him as though they were two halves of the same whole. One large hand slid around, settling at the base of her spine and warming her skin through the thin material of her dress. The other held her hand in a proper dance hold level with his shoulder.

As they swayed to the music, Lucie fought her duplicitous impulses of kissing him madly and stomping on his foot before exiting the ballroom.

"You just spent an awful lot of money to get something you claimed you didn't even want," she finally said.

"I know."

She studied him, trying to solve the puzzle without having to ask for the answers, but the normal clues were absent. There was no smug smile. No jaw muscle jumping in irritation. Not a disapproving frown or even a challenging hitch of one brow. For the first time ever, Reid Andrews was utterly unreadable.

"Why?"

"Because you refused to take my calls, and I know you're too honorable to back out of a date that some poor schmuck has shelled out an exorbitant amount of money for."

Averting her eyes she said, "So this is all fun and games to you. That's comforting."

"Hell, no, this isn't a game." With the tips of his fingers he brought her face front and center. "I had to see you. Damn, I've missed you, sweetheart."

Air. She needed air.

Spinning on her heel she weaved an erratic path through the dancing couples to where she knew French doors opened onto a large patio and manicured gardens. Lucie expected he'd follow her, but she didn't care so long as she got away from the crowd and their prying eyes. She refused to break down in front of her colleagues and their guests.

Pushing through the doors she inhaled the bouquet of floral scents deep into her lungs before letting it out as she crossed to the large three-tiered fountain at the entrance to the gardens. Crossing her arms over her middle she held tight as though she could prevent losing herself to her own emotions.

She heard the gravel crunch under his shoes as he came to stand behind her, but he remained silent as she watched the water cascade in front of her. When he finally spoke, his low voice coiled around her body, adding strength to her embrace, easing some of her tension. "That dress looks stunning on you. You're the most magnificent woman I've ever laid eyes on."

Lucie said nothing. She couldn't even if she'd wanted to. Her throat was locked up tight. She heard a slight scratching sound, like sandpaper, and pictured him rubbing his jawline.

"I regained my belt. I beat Diaz."

"I know," she said softly.

No matter how many times she told herself she wouldn't watch his fight, she'd known anything short of nuclear war wouldn't prevent her from seeing it. Sitting on her couch with her knees drawn into her chest and her teeth gnawing the hell out of her lip, Lucie had observed every excruciating moment. Of course it'd been too much to ask for a quick bout. No, she'd been subjected to almost three full rounds of watching Reid take blows and kicks to his head and body that looked like they could take down a gorilla. Thankfully, he gave just as good as he got, and in the third round he managed to knock out his opponent with a spectacular head kick.

She'd never been so relieved in her life. Or so proud.

Stop daydreaming and say something, damn you. She cleared her throat and said what she supposed was the logical response. "Congratulations. You're once again the champion…just as you wanted all along."

"Not all along." A finger trailed lightly from her shoulder to elbow in excruciating slowness. "My goals and ambitions have changed considerably since I walked into your office that day."

She shook her head. That's not what he claimed a month ago when she opened herself up to him more than she'd done with anyone else.

"Lucie, I retired after my fight."

She spun around and stared at him with wide eyes. "Why would you do that? You won."

"It didn't matter if I won or lost. I made the decision to retire before the fight, no matter the outcome."

"But," she stammered, "what will you do?"

"There's more I can do with my life besides fighting. I was thinking I could move back here and try something else. Maybe pursue my sculpting, or buy hideous argyle clothing and take up golf. I don't care what I do, as long as I'm with you."

She was shaking her head before he even finished. "No. That's what you say now, but eventually you're going to feel that itch, that need, and at your age, if you're out of the circuit it's going to be so hard to get back in. You can't quit because of me, Reid. You can't put that kind of pressure on me."

"Whoa, slow down, sweetheart," he said, grasping her firmly by her shoulders and making sure he had her full attention before starting again. "I'm not quitting, I'm retiring. And I'm not doing it because of you. I'm doing it for me."

"I don't understand. You *love* to fight."

Reid took her hands in his, bringing them between them, rubbing his thumbs over the backs of her fingers. "Remember when I told you that I'd always love the sport, but wouldn't always love being in it?"

"Yes. You said it after dinner that night."

"That's what this is. My heart's just not in it anymore."

His eyes searched hers as though hoping to see that she understood, but she wasn't sure she did. "Then where is it?"

"With you, Lucie. My heart is with you."

She wanted so desperately to just go with what he was telling her, but a big part of her—the part that had been crushed a month ago when he walked away from her—held her back, warning her about false hopes. She needed more validation than that.

"Since when?" she challenged.

"Since when has my heart been with you?" She nodded. He stepped closer and framed her face in his large hands. "Quite possibly from the first time I heard you snort." He placed a kiss on the tip of her nose. "Very probably when you flirted with our waiter." A warm kiss on the freckle by her eye. "Almost certainly the first time you fell asleep in my arms." A small kiss on the opposite cheek. "And most definitely the night we made love." Finally, a tender kiss on the lips.

How was it possible for one man to be so many different things? Fighter, makeover expert, professional seducer, artist, and now poet. A woman didn't stand a chance against a combination like that. He was nothing she'd thought she needed in a man, and yet everything she wanted and more.

Rising on her toes, she threw her arms around his neck and kissed him for everything she was worth. Strong arms banded around her, holding her tight against him as he branded her with searing lips. Somewhere nearby the bells of a church chimed a lighthearted melody as they at last came up for air.

Catching her breath she made one final request. "Say it, Reid."

He grinned. "You're going to make me spell it out, aren't you?"

"You're lucky I don't make you write it in the sky with one of those little planes."

He chuckled, but sobered fairly quickly. Still holding her close, he touched his forehead to hers and spoke with the utmost sincerity shining in his hazel eyes. "Lucie Marie Maris…I am completely and utterly in love with you. And as God is my witness—no matter how long it takes—someday I will be worthy enough to be your husband, because I can't bear the thought of living without you."

The bells started tolling the midnight hour in slow gongs as she soaked up the beautiful words that acted as a balm to her soul, repairing the rift he'd caused weeks earlier. She felt whole again and, for the first time in her adult life, unconditionally loved.

Her chin quivered as she tried to hold back the tears rushing to her eyes, but it was no use. They spilled over her cheeks, one after another, and she'd be lucky if her sooty tears didn't drip onto her dress and ruin it. Stupid man.

"Now look what you've gone and done." She sniffled, determined to at least keep snot out of the whole train wreck that was previously her carefully applied makeup. "A simple 'I love you' would have sufficed."

He smiled before placing a gentle kiss on her lips. "I love you."

"It's too late, I'm already a mess."

"I think you're gorgeous."

Lucie squinched up her nose. "You're biased. I can't go back in there like this."

He canted his head to the side for a moment, and then smiled down at her. "The clock's about to strike twelve, Cinderella. I should probably get you up to the safety of my hotel room. You know, just in case."

She gave a short laugh, using the back of a hand to swipe at the black streaks under her eyes and holding it up as proof. "I'm fairly sure I've already turned back into my former state, but getting out of this dress and into a hot bath sounds like heaven."

His eyes darkened with intensity and a muscle

in his jaw ticked. She hadn't meant her statement to sound sexual, but clearly that's how it was received judging by Reid's reaction.

Grabbing her hand, he nearly growled and said, "I couldn't agree more."

Without waiting another second, he spun, pulling her out of the garden toward the front of the hotel. His strides were so long and quick she had to hitch up her dress and jog behind him to keep up. Amazingly enough she was managing the pace just fine when suddenly the heel of her right shoe became trapped in a crevice, causing her to falter as her foot continued on without it. Thankfully Reid used his lightning-fast reflexes to catch her before she face-planted on the paving stones near the French doors.

Unable to help herself, she laughed hysterically as she reached down and tried to wrench it free. A couple of rough tugs freed her shoe...but not the heel. Mouth agape she stared at the stubborn spike still wedged in the stone. "Well, crap. Doesn't that just figure."

He swept her up into his arms, took one look at her bare foot and said, "Well now it's official."

She wrapped her arms around his neck, her broken footwear dangling from the fingers of one hand. "What's official?"

"You really are Cinderella."

"Well, in that case…" Lucie caught her lower lip between her teeth, traced the tan skin revealed by the open V of his shirt, then glanced up coyly through her lashes, just like he'd taught her. "…let's get started on our Happily Ever After."

As the last chime faded into the starry night, he met her gaze with a heart-melting smile and said, "As you wish, princess," before carrying her off to do just that.